Stalin's

Zdena Tomin was born in 1941 in Prague. Like many of her contemporaries, she has led a 'subversive' life. She started writing surrealist poetry in 1959, when surrealism was a prohibited art in Czechoslovakia, graduated in philosophy and sociology and published short stories and essays in the sixties. She was then placed on the list of authors banned for life after the final downfall of Dubcek's regime.

Charter 77 brought a new inspiration: she wrote a novella and a play for the hand-typed 'samizdat', *Padlock*. In 1979 she became one of Charter 77's spokespersons, an involvement which meant intense harassment for her and her family. In 1980, she travelled to Oxford with her husband, philosopher Julius Tomin: nine months later they were both deprived of their Czech citizenship as 'enemies of the State' and became refugees in Britain.

Zdena Tomin now lives in London with her two sons.

EF.

STALIN'S SHOE

Zdena Tomin

J. M. Dent & Sons Ltd
London Melbourne

First published in Great Britain by Century Hutchinson Ltd, 1986
This paperback edition first published by J. M. Dent & Sons Ltd, 1987
Copyright © Zdena Tomin 1986

Printed in Great Britain by Guernsey Press Co. Ltd., Guernsey, C.I.
for J. M. Dent & Sons Ltd
Aldine House, 33 Welbeck Street, London W1M 8LX

British Library Cataloguing in Publication Data

Tomin, Zdena
  Stalin's shoe.
  I. Title
  823′.914[F]   PR6070.04/
  ISBN 0–460–02470–1

The author admits that she has borrowed extensively from life,
her own and other people's. The resulting characters, however –
apart from that of Joseph Stalin – are figments of her imagination
and must not be mistaken for real persons, dead or alive.

Ozymandias

I met a traveller from an antique land
Who said: Two vast and trunkless legs of stone
Stand in the desert . . . Near them, on the sand,
Half sunk, a shattered visage lies, whose frown,
And wrinkled lip, and sneer of cold command,
Tell that its sculptor well those passions read
Which yet survive, stamped on these lifeless things,
The hand that mocked them, and the heart that fed:
And on the pedestal these words appear:
'My name is Ozymandias, king of kings:
Look on my works, ye Mighty, and despair!'
Nothing beside remains. Round the decay
Of that colossal wreck, boundless and bare
The lone and level sands stretch far away.

PERCY BYSSHE SHELLEY

1792–1822

A thousand thanks to my friends and family – small in numbers but great in endurance – for their patience, generosity and humour in upholding me, in so many moments both of tiresome *ennui d' exile*, and genuine anguish. They know who they are: I shall keep their names close to my heart.

Very special thanks to those wider organizations which allowed me to participate in their concerns, in particular to European Nuclear Disarmament, and to the Transnational Institute, which has provided me with material support for the past year and a half.

Thanks also to Hutchinson for taking the risk with a Czech attempting – heretically and erratically – to write in English, especially to Anthony Whittome whose gentle touch has carried me through the worst of doubts.

Before the reader, who has not turned this book down, I stand humble, excited and grateful.

Zdena Tomin

1

'One night, just as we left the cemetery gate, my mother, dressed all in black for one of those family funerals, gave me a strong push from behind. Although less unfriendly than usual, it sent me flying across the road.

' "Don't look back!" my mother called after me in her strictest voice. She then walked under a passing lorry, and died.

'I went home very slowly, growing older and heavier until, on our doorstep, I squatted down and gave birth to a very small baby girl or rather a miniature woman with a curiously old face. My mother, now wearing a crisp white apron over her funeral clothes, stooped over me very disapprovingly and took the baby away to wherever she came from.

'I was left aching with want of love, and a coldness spreading inside me. When I woke up, I couldn't get warm for hours.'

Dr B. has been treating Linda Wren for psychosomatic pains in her back, chest and head for many weeks now, without much success and with the additional complication of an undesirable attachment. When she came to see him on her forty-fourth birthday, he finally told her the story of a Russian surgeon who found that his appendix was about to burst: at the time he was on a polar expedition, and iced in. To save his life the man had operated on himself, using a set of mirrors held high by his shipmates.

'Amazing,' said Dr B., 'but it can be done. I suppose the trickiest task is to keep your scalpel steady.'

Astonished, Linda thought: he is washing his hands of me!

'Does it mean that you don't want me to come any more?' she asked, and added: 'I am not a Russian, you know.'

Dr B. coughed. 'Dear Linda, all I mean is – why don't we give the couch a rest? For a couple of months, shall we say? Then, maybe, you will want to come back to me. And maybe you won't.'

'I should miss you, John. I liked you a lot, I—'

Dr B. shook his head reproachfully and his fingers began to drum brief rhythms on the desk.

Linda bit her lip. 'Could I have my dreams back, please?' she said politely.

'By all means. Let me photocopy them, it won't take a minute.'

'I'd rather you didn't, if you don't mind.' Linda blushed.

Dr B. pushed a thin file across the desk. 'Here you are, then. But I don't think you are being fair. You must know what important research material dreams are for me. You take everything too personally, my dear, you are too intense; but then I suppose you can't help it.'

Linda rose hastily. She did not want to hear *that* one again. Dr B. shook hands with her and then, following a regrettable impulse, kissed her on the mouth.

'My dear Linda, why don't you go away for a while? I would if I could. London gets everybody down at this time of year. A little chalet in the French Alps would do you more good than I could at the moment.'

Acting on another extravagant impulse, he added: 'You needn't pay for your last sessions, dear. Have them on me. A birthday present.'

'Thank you,' said Linda, her cheeks burning.

'And keep on writing,' Dr B. called after her. 'Maybe you'll let me see your dreams again, some time?'

Outside, the sun was shining but the streets were dark after a vehement February shower. On Euston Road a cold wind thrashed about in all directions. Several blown-off hats were rolling on the pavement. Linda caught hers just in time, but the file slid from under her arm and landed empty in a black puddle several yards away. The white sheets of paper were tossed high in the wind and flapped against lamp posts and the windscreens of passing cars, until finally they became indistinguishable from the rest of the city's dirt. Two of them were recovered by an agile and helpful young man, obviously an employee of the branch of Barclays Bank on the corner. He expressed his sympathy and hoped that the papers were not of an irreplaceable nature?

'Not at all,' said Linda, 'but thank you very much.'

Linda's shoes were soon soaked through and she was shivering. Using the two sheets of paper as a flag, she hailed a cab.

'Elia Street, Islington,' she said, and had to repeat it twice. 'Off Colebrooke Row,' she explained, and for some reason the driver winked and grinned at her.

The afternoon light was so bright and clear that it had a magnifying effect. The sections of the streets upon which it dwelled came out in overwhelming detail; the shadows cast by buildings and trees and even people were huge and dark, a succession of sharply defined blackouts.

'I often dream of landscapes, sculptured, wondrous ones with patches of snow and richly detailed vegetation, and with waters either wild or completely quiet under shining surfaces. They are happy dreams provided they remain silent, without a word spoken.

'Last night, I had another such well-shaped dream. I was walking upstream on a river bank, the water was rushing by, sometimes under, sometimes over a footbridge of bright red stone. Daffodils grew on trees like orchids and made me laugh. I did some jumping and leaping, and soon entered the roofless ruin of an abbey. It was obviously a wrong thing to have done and I was anxious to leave, but a telephone rang, shaking the old wall so violently that I had no choice but to answer it. It was my mother. She spoke to me in English, well, a kind of English.

' "Mother, you don't speak English! You never did!", I cried. There was a moment of silence before she laughed. She laughed and laughed in her merriest way, but when I joined in, the phone went dead. I woke up choking with that cut-off laughter!'

Linda tore the two sheets of paper into small strips and, when she thought that the driver wasn't looking, she threw them out of the window.

Further north, the traffic eased up and the cab was moving fairly quickly. The rhythm of light-shadow-light became unbearably swift and Linda had to close her eyes.

'Where are you from, love?' asked the driver over his shoulder.

Linda kept her eyes shut and pretended not to hear.

'You've got an accent there, you know – okay, let me guess. How about – Guernsey, eh? – You can't be from Australia, can you! – Friendly, aren't you, love! Are you a feminist? You look like one, you know. Sour-like.'

Hating herself, Linda gave him a tip.

'Had too much to drink, haven't we, love,' he said and took off, scoring maximum points.

The house that Alice, Ruth and Linda shared in Elia Street had that slightly dilapidated look which is supposed to be cheerful.

Alice was down with flu and had decided to have it on the sofa in the lounge. Ruth was running up and down the stairs to keep her in hot tea and lemon.

'Happy birthday,' she greeted Linda a little breathlessly. 'You do look awful again!'

'What is the matter now?' growled Alice, and blew her nose ostentatiously.

'Nothing. Just a pig of a cab driver, that's all.'

It was beginning to look like one of those evenings when they lived on top of each other.

Ruth, delightfully absurd and absurdly feminine with her big fuzzy hair and her tiny figure, was a make-up artist with

London Weekend Television. She lived on the first floor, next to the large bathroom which she treated as her workshop.

Alice, who was uncommonly tall but strikingly handsome, was a compulsive painter; she lived in the top floor studio-bedroom, but needed the lounge, too, to get away from it all.

Looking at her beautiful body stretched along the entire length of the sofa, and at her cheeks dark against the pillow, Linda felt that old pang of jealousy again. Once, when Alice was going on and on about how she loved dear little Ruth, Linda swallowed her pride and asked whether Alice loved her, too. Alice was silent for an entire evil minute . . . after which Linda said something feeble and fled downstairs.

Linda Wren used to be a part-time lecturer at University College, specializing in European literature in general and Franz Kafka in particular, but she had been the first to go when the department tightened its belt. Now she was merely a freelance this and a freelance that, and, appropriately, occupied the small and dark bedroom next to the kitchen in the basement.

There were only five birthday cards on the mantelpiece. But one of them was from Paris, from Linda's pretty twenty-one-year-old daughter who was studying in France with her mother's blessings and on her father's allowance; Linda re-read it and put a smile on her face.

Ruth had been waiting for some such signal: she immediately brought in the birthday cake. Alice decided that she was not so terribly ill after all, and would have a glass or two of the *méthode champenoise*. Somehow she felt reassured that her own daughter, who was nineteen and had just left to seek her fortunes in New York after three nerve-racking years on the dole in Islington, would not forget her mother's birthday either, when the time came. Alice had never been married, while Linda was divorced and Ruth a widow, but she thought that she had possibly been a better mother than either of the two.

11

Ruth's little Prudence was thirteen, and the fact that she was in an expensive girls' school in Somerset, the fees having been paid from the money her father left in trust for her, was something of a litmus paper in the household.

If all was well among them, the three women agreed that independent schooling was the best and only possibility for a bright young thing like Prudence, and to hell with their weepy socialist conscience. If all was not well, Ruth became defensive or aggressive about it, and they all disagreed with each other, although they were not consistent in their attitudes, and would swop them around from argument to argument.

And if the worst came to the worst, Ruth and Alice would turn against Linda.

'Shut up, Strizlik,' they would say, 'as if you could understand!'

Střízlík had been the name of Linda's Czech father, and – by an absolutely mad coincidence – her English husband's too, only stripped of the Czech accents. It was the name that was printed on her British passport, but because *strizlik* meant nothing more than 'wren', that little brown bird with a far-fetching voice, Linda preferred to call and sign herself Wren.

When all was well between them, Ruth and Alice found it a reasonable precaution.

Ruth believed in birthdays, funerals and fate in general. She liked to think that dates and places of birth and death had a special meaning in life. Alice vigorously denied all predestination, as well as her own preoccupation with class and religion. She claimed that she belonged to none; only people from the working classes had that privilege; Ruth and Linda would never understand.

Linda usually kept to fairly abstract levels in such discussions; tonight, perhaps because it was her birthday, perhaps because she was so disconsolate, she feebly protested:

'But I was born in a working-class family too, Alice.'

'For goodness' sake, Strizlik,' exclaimed Alice, 'that's different!'

Soon afterwards Alice fell asleep on the sofa and was snoring away in bubbly little chortles. Ruth and Linda were playing Scrabble for a while, but Linda was winning and Ruth was a bad loser. They had an argument about the word 'Prague'. Ruth wouldn't have it while Linda insisted that it was a perfectly good English word because in Czech it was actually spelled 'Praha'.

'Really, Linda,' complained Ruth, 'what's come over you? Alice was right, you are being such a Strizlik tonight!'

The miniature clock on the mantelpiece struck midnight, and chimed a whining, petulant tune. Linda wanted to smash it, throw it to the floor and thump it to pieces. It was her life that was whining away in that fussy incongruous mechanism! A phoney life; an intricate wire-mesh structure erected over an exhausted pit. Yet there must be a live lump of coal somewhere, burning itself out: Linda could feel a wave of heat seeping upwards right now. She blinked with tears.

'Oh dear, oh dear,' sighed Ruth. 'Nobody loves you, is that it? How many times have I told you that if you don't play the game, you can't win! You could be quite attractive if only you tried. Look at yourself! The stuff you're wearing! Your hair! The way you sit, like a rolled-up hedgehog! I give up. I think you ought to go into psychotherapy or something. See a shrink. But don't tell him where you come from, or he'd be far too easy on you. That's your trouble, you know. There is nothing so special about you – it's just plain middle-aged misery. Yet you always hint that there is. It scares people away. *And* it's boring.'

Linda did not tell her about Dr B., or how she snatched her dreams from him only to see them gone with the wind. She promised to have a look at herself, and Ruth was pleased.

Together, they tucked Alice in carefully, switched the lights off and then they went to bed themselves, Ruth upstairs, Linda downstairs.

For months Linda had avoided mirrors wherever possible. She was always on the lookout for them, in public places and other people's homes, for she dreaded to be caught unawares and confronted with an image of herself which she refused to accept as having anything to do with her inner self and would spoil her day or evening out. Her own mirror she approached with conscious care, her mouth set and her chin up, holding her stomach in and her shoulders straight. She would concentrate only on details in her face, and for the shortest time necessary to apply a token make-up. She tried to look herself in the eyes most of the time. The eyes were fine; she recognized them as her own.

Tonight, however, she had to know.

She went to the mirror with her eyes shut, said a little prayer, and looked.

Staring at her was a hapless creature lost in flesh; a half-melted face with a greyish skin, slack mouth and a soft chin which seemed to have no bone at all; eyes blurred as if covered with cobwebs.

Mother, something cried in her, Mother, didn't you say, when you rubbed my cheeks and mouth with a rough, wet towel before sending me to school, didn't you say that a woman's soul was in her face?

Towards dawn, Linda slept a little. A thousand fingers tugged and pulled at some loose straps in her brain. She had inarticulate, hurried dreams.

She couldn't have slept more than a couple of hours, but she woke up feeling suddenly larger than life. She went into the kitchen and stood by the garden door. The day outside was heavy, the clarity of the air had gone; rain was coming, probably weeks of it.

Linda had always loved rain: now she was overwhelmed by a passionate desire to get as near to it as she possibly could. To get to a place where you could raise your arm and touch the cloud: become a part of it. Any passionate desire was in itself a godsend, an unexpected blessing, a release. Linda could not remember when she last felt passionate and what it was she desired; impatiently, she gave up trying. It wasn't important, what *was* important was how to fulfil the present desire; it needed cunning and determination. She braced herself.

She knew a place. She'd been there once with the white-haired Professor Owen who sat through her lecture on Kafka shaking his head and making her tremendously nervous. Afterwards he came to tell her how much he'd enjoyed it. She had a thing or two quite wrong, he said, but it was obvious that she loved the man Kafka and knew his Prague; he wanted more of it. What was she doing for Easter? Would she mind spending it in North Wales? He had to go up there. The *hafodty*, the cottage that is, had remained empty for the whole of the winter, his wife being ill and all that, and it might need a touch of repair. But how silly of him, she would want to be with her family. . . . No family, Linda had said quickly, no family to be with. We've grown . . . independent.

In the event, things hadn't worked out well. The old Land Rover had got stuck halfway down the track leading to the cottage, and they had had to carry their stuff – food, books and a bag of coal – a good half a mile; the professor had strained his back and was very irritable. It had rained most of the time, and while Linda loved the rain, it made him grumpier than ever.

But the place! Wild and gentle, gentle and wild, rough mountains shielding its back and sides, its front overlooking miles and miles of down-sloping hills and the shimmer and shine of the sea below in clear weather, and overlooking nothing when the clouds came down to touch the grass.

By eight-thirty, while Ruth and Alice were still firmly asleep, Linda had spoken to Professor Owen on the telephone; she had had to overcome his considerable reluctance, but in the end she obtained his permission.

'The key is in the shed,' he had said. 'It hangs behind the blind mirror. But I still wish you wouldn't, at this time of year. . . .'

15

By ten she was on a train to Blaenau Ffestiniog, via Llandudno Junction. Blind mirror, she was whispering to herself, blind mirror hiding a key!

By eight at night a farmer on the lookout for early lambs had found her, soaked and exhausted, sitting on a large rucksack in the middle of a narrow lane behind Tan-y-Bwlch. She had walked five miles and was overjoyed to get a ride for two of the remaining three. He didn't speak to her and she tiredly thought that he too disapproved of her. But when he set her down at the gate on the top of the track he helped her to put the rucksack on and thrust a small torch into her hand, pointing to the pitch-dark outline of the young forest she had to go through.

'*Diolch mawr*,' said Linda and the farmer spat. There was no malice or disrespect to it – it simply marked the end of an encounter with a woman who might, just might, have been a witch.

The magic of the blind mirror had worked. There was indeed a key.

When it became clear that Linda Wren had disappeared from London, there was much bitterness in the small world she had inhabited. Ruth and Alice and a few other friends felt misunderstood and mistreated; betrayed. There were also some articles and lectures Linda had promised and did not deliver, and people who were therefore inclined to think of her as, well, ungrateful.

Apart from the brief note Linda had left in the kitchen, there was only one more communication with the house in Elia Street, a postcard which arrived much later on April Fools' Day: Alice tore it up. She and Ruth would have preferred to believe that Linda had been kidnapped and dragged into the depths of the Russian empire. A postcard from Wales about an owl, a couple of friendly bats and a magpie barking deep into the sunset was a profound disappointment.

16

Linda's daughter in Paris had had an unusual number of letters from her mother throughout the spring. They arrived in twos and threes and the envelopes were all crumpled and smudged, but the letters themselves were short and quietly funny, about wild flowers and shapes of clouds and lambs and flocks of hungry rooks; the very last one was about big black cattle shitting loudly under the cottage's window at dawn.

The girl was pleased both with the letters and with the fact that she didn't have to write back, as there was never a return address.

Not knowing exactly why he should bother, Dr B. decided to give Linda yet another session and perhaps a lunch afterwards. He rang the number in Elia Street only to be told by a peevish female voice that Linda had gone up to Wales. Where exactly, nobody seemed to know. Why, was an even greater mystery. And unless somebody was paying for it, there was no way she could afford a holiday. She had not been doing very well lately, and could not pay even her full share of the bills. 'Maybe you know more about this than we do,' said the voice with sudden suspicion, and he hung up.

He fretted and fumed until he received a short note which Linda had scribbled and posted at Euston Station before her departure.

'Dear Dr B.,' it said, 'I have taken your advice and am leaving London for a chalet in Wales. I intend to keep my scalpel steady but the mirrors are blind, or so I hope. Thank you for your generosity, and please give the couch a pat.

Yours in haste

Linda W.

PS Sorry for craving your affection so much. Maybe you shouldn't have encouraged me to call you John. Sorry if you think me ungrateful. L.'

'Sorry!' Dr B. exclaimed, re-read the note and frowned. 'Chalet, my foot. Some ghastly cold forsaken place in Wales, at this time of year!'

But he felt strangely relieved. Ten days later, a long letter arrived from Linda Wren. He read it several times, and each time he felt more and more like Ruth and Alice: misunderstood and mistreated. In addition, he was painfully aware that he was getting old, and growing tired and weary of women.

What Linda had not remembered was that the cottage sat in a shallow depression surrounded by trees. For a full view of the mountains and the valley and the sea down in the south, she had to walk ahead some thirty yards, up a gentle slope at the top of which was a smooth grey rock.

It was a perfect rock for a lookout. Seen from the neighbouring meadows, or indeed from just below, it revealed a shape from Linda's past that was both peculiar and familiar. Stalin's left shoe, that's what it looked like! Right size, right colour, the same kind of stone, everything. Never mind that the rest of the Generalissimo was missing; weather permitting, Linda would spend many a happy hour sitting in that comfortable instep scribbling her pages or simply gazing at the horizon, just as she had done ages and ages ago, on the Letna hill in Prague.

The truth is that when Linda Strizlik/Wren finished her pages, her mother turned in her grave for the last time; at which the universe heaved a sigh of relief.

2

Dear Dr B.,

I have not fooled you with the chalet, have I; and I could not fool you now if I said that the cleansing powers of nature worked wonders with me straight away, that I have become a better person from the moment I set foot on my mountain. I like to think of it as mine but of course it isn't, the dense young woods belong to the forestry, the grasslands on the hills belong to an enterprising woman farmer who will soon bring her cattle in from her farm some eight miles away, and the old *hafodty* belongs to a professor of European literature whose focus on Franz Kafka made it morally impossible for him not to surrender the key of the place to me.

Hafodty, my dear civilized Dr B., means a summer dwelling of shepherds, and although it is built of solid bulging rocks and irregular slate blocks that make you marvel at just how muscular the old Welsh people were, in February it is as wet and cold inside as it is outside.

You can easily guess what happened after I arrived, with all my old miseries in the bag: I crept into bed and stayed there, shivering under a heap of wet blankets, never leaving it but to drink and pass water. Existing, as a human, only in feverish and increasingly irrelevant dreams.

But that is my problem, isn't it, that I am so irrelevant, so unrelated to things that matter in the present.

In the last of those dreams, I was fleeing from a doomed city into which I was brought as a slave to work in a barber's shop. I ran down a narrow valley alongside a stream until I reached a small bakery, went in and shut the door.

Through its glass pane, I looked up the valley expecting nothing less than a mushroom cloud. Instead, a single grey hair, a woman's hair, was floating down from where the city was, turning golden in the process, shining like a solitary ray of sun. There was such an urgency in it I could have cried; I tried so hard to work out the meaning of it, that I woke up.

I can see you smile, doctor. Of course you are right; it was the bakery that did it, that tossed me out of lethargy. I hadn't eaten for days! I stumbled into the kitchen and ate a canful of cold baked beans, and started a new life. My fireplace is gleaming bright now, and I am no longer startled by every sound at night. The high cruising of buzzards, and even a mid-air fight between a raven and a peregrine, I read as good omens.

But the purpose of this letter is not to boast. I want to ask your forgiveness, dear Dr B., for what I am going to do.

I am going to borrow your name and your general physique, in particular the outline of your shoulders, neck and head, some of the deep lines in your face, the strong angles of your forehead and nose, and the shape and colour of your eyes as they were when you kissed me. I am going to reassemble these features into another man, John, a man I can easily imagine loving and being kindly, distantly loved by him.

I have, you may remember, no religious faith. But even if I had, I doubt it would be proper to treat Him as a distant lover. Yet I have to have one, at least for the time being, at least until I find out why on earth I am so tortured by womanhood.

My back still hurts, doctor, and I get these burning pains in the chest from time to time, but there is absolutely no headache.

Dear, dear Dr B., when I last saw you, I could tell by the shift in your voice how glad you were to get rid of me. My lack of progress must have been hurtful to your professional standards, and those dreadful declarations of love I made to you just had to be simply revolting.

So please remember that there are no strings attached any more; the man John I am now clinging to is carving necks of violins high up in Scotland, or selling hand-painted post-cards in the Quartier Latin, or fishing in Arctic waters. In any case, he is entirely mine.

Yours thankfully.

L.

3

Dear John,

Travelling on a train just before Christmas, sliding through a wet world of pearl greys and dull greens and yellows, between Stroud and Kemble I have suddenly discovered a long valley of my youth. Of the time, that is, when my daughter was small and her father and I took her out of town for long walks almost every Sunday, holding hands. . . .

Everything was in its place: the old chaffed houses on steep slopes, the shabby little factories with brick chimneys falling down and the metallic ones rusty, the clustered back-yards, the weed-infested streams, the magnificent old water-mill, the long yellow grasses sweeping over the timid yet everlasting lawns, the little lake frozen around the edges, the two lonely roads winding upwards, the graceful beechwoods scaling the hillsides with their leafless trees looking slim and youthful. Not a living soul in sight and for the last mile or two not even a solitary house or a horse, only the long sweep of heartache. I walked through that valley so many times, on so many winter days – and yet I couldn't have done so.

At Swindon, I changed trains. Anxious to break the spell, I asked a young man whether this was indeed the platform the London train would come to.

'I wouldn't know, would I,' he said and added, his hand-some face sullen: 'Never been here before. Not in my life.'

'No,' I almost whispered, 'Neither have I.'

'So there,' he concluded wistfully, and when the train came and left and I looked out of the window he was still standing on the platform, apparently having no intention to make a journey.

Oh, but I will. Backwards, at first; but who knows, maybe there is symmetry in life and at a certain point, backwards or forwards does not matter.

I'll have you to help me along, won't I.

Yours shyly

L.

Dear John,

My watch stopped long ago and time is soft and yielding. I can't begin to tell you what a pleasure it is to know that you exist in these same mellow rhythms! I have loved before – even if it seems ages ago – and timing was always a problem.

How can two people walk hand in hand and heart in heart on those hair-raising ridges of hours, minutes and seconds, how can they possibly synchronize? God knows I tried; I mean by adapting to my beloved's pace; but it never worked.

That, and my damnable inability to share a bed. It may have something to do with the crowded conditions of my childhood, but there is more to it. You see, I never sleep, I never fall into a blessed oblivion to wake up refreshed and ready to live on. I wake up exhausted, I need to eat a dinner in the morning and have a few hours' rest before I can tackle the waking part of my life. My dreams are not pleasant or unpleasant drifts or cleansing binges of the subconscious; they are a hard, active living in an uncompromising universe which is both of my and its own making; a very dangerous and seductive territory.

Maybe this is why I have aged so quickly, I practically lead a double life! But it is certainly the main reason why I cannot share a bed, I cannot risk an intrusion and the distinct possibility that I could hurt the intruder; I need absolute freedom of action.

But how does one say it to a lover? The only way is to invent some slightly embarrassing disorder, some physical frailty, or some theory of how damaging actually sharing a bed can be for a creative sexual relationship. And he'll still believe that you don't love him truly; mutual friends will shake their heads and spread rumours and the odd woman will edge in for a supposed vacancy; you end up believing it yourself and vacate the post of love.

None of this with you, dear John. You understand what I understand, and wherever I stumble and fall you are there, not to protect, but to share the pain. You laugh when I laugh, but you are your own man as well as mine, I can tell because the mere idea of you fills me with quiet desire.

Like this morning, I went about my simple chores with a lingering image of your eyelashes: they were almost white from sun and funny to touch, so vibrant and rather scratchy, not soft or silky at all. Little currents of delight made my lips twitch, and I felt erotic without a trace of shame; for an hour or so, years of sourness were lifted from me.

Dear John,

Clouds are still heavy in the south-east, but in the north and west the sky is a clear pale blue. The peak of Y Wyddfa is glittering with snow, while the two Moelwyn mountains, Bach and Fawr, stand already washed black and barren. Rooks and carrion crows fly high today, but from time to time there is a deep bark in the sky and a pair of ravens come soaring low, making the scattered sheep bleat out loud. Meadow pipits are combing the air whistling like mad, glorious wheatears perch on boulders warmed by the sun, and from the tufts of last year's moor-grass by the stream come the babblings of a curlew. I have to walk lightly not to injure a primrose, already in flower but still close to the ground. It is March, John, March, and I feel as shy and as curious as a newborn lamb.

I am beginning to believe that there is a future for you and me, dear John; but of course there are stoneweights of memories to go through, sorting out rot from root; picking the bones clean. I am going to write it down for you as I go, for I am no good at other means of communication so far. I wish I could paint or make music, but I am just a heavy-footed literary brute.

L.

Poor Emily

Poor Emily, little Linda's mother! Quick Street in Prague is only half a mile long and as peaceful as can be, though there is a war raging through the world; everybody knows everybody in the old four-storey tenements; the one car in the whole street is kept safely in a garage, so everybody's children play on the street where old women keep an angry eye on them; yet there is no end to poor Emily's worries.

But then her little Linda is a cunning brat, three, four years old. She disappears and reappears in her own time and you can't get a word out of her.

'Where have you been, Linda, you wretched child? Your mother's been worried sick about you!'

'Nowhere,' she would say and grin all over her dirty face.

'I don't know,' she would whisper, and you could see smudged traces of tears on her cheeks, though you'd never catch her actually crying.

Every other night between suppertime and bedtime, through dusk and nightfall, poor Emily is standing on the pavement, her arms crossed on her stomach under a spotless apron, her face twisted between worry, wrath and the friendliness she always keeps for her neighbours – while her two elder children lead a search party for the brat.

Lunchtime searches have been abandoned as it gradually becomes clear that when not at home, little Linda lunches off somebody else's table, paying her way by telling astonishing stories and singing breathless little songs she makes up on the spot. Small children are easily fed when Linda's there, as their mouths hang open and their eyes are averted from the unappetizing wartime food; so nobody really minds the shameless little beggar. Poor Emily minds, she is very proud, but there is nothing she can do.

At night, Linda is never found until she decides to come forward herself, but a search party is always dispatched to keep up appearances; this is a nice respectable neighbourhood even if most families are poorer than church mice.

By some gentle joke of Providence, most of the family names are taken from birds: Sojka/Jay, Vrabec/Sparrow,

Špaček/Starling, Hrdliška/Dove, Kačer/Drake, Laštuvka/Swallow, Střízlík/Wren.

If they are not, there is usually something wrong with the people: the Beránek/Lamb family all wear loud clothes and receive strange visitors at night; Mrs Pokorná/Humble sends her daughter to piano and ballet lessons!

Poor Emily never spanks Linda, though she well ought to; nor does she ever hug her for that matter. It's as if she had a profound distaste for touching the child. And Václav Střízlík/Wren, little Linda's father (a good chap, a bit soft in the head perhaps) simply dotes on the brat, it is pitiful to watch.

When Emily herself was little, she was as clever as they come, she had a sharp mind and a small compact body that took any amount of hard work in its stride, and she was the neatest and most diligent child that ever attended the village school for five consecutive winters. She wanted to become a teacher herself, she wanted it more than anything else; but as the eldest of six daughters of an impoverished farmer, she never stood a chance. There was a rich uncle who owned the fattest fields stretching from the village to the river and beyond to the very edge of the forest, and he owned a good chunk of that too, but he did not believe in pampering poor relations and never went beyond lending them a team of old horses now and then. Emily was fourteen and hardly taller than a ten-year-old boy when she was sent off to a town some thirty miles away to become a maid in a villa.

She went without remorse, intending to better herself in any way she could. The villa belonged to an Austro-Hungarian, the owner of a prospering factory; he had piled up a neat little fortune by producing high-quality tiles out of white Bohemian kaolin sands, but he preferred the good cultured life to the hard toils of a capitalist, and did not expand. His wife was fragile, and he was soon deeply grateful to young Emily for being able to cope with all the whining and whimpering and romantic pinings of the *gnädige Frau*; in four years Emily, who had grown up into a presentable girl, was given some new chic clothes and was acting as his wife's companion on frequent travels to Vienna or Prague, while in the villa she continued to be a maid and a cook and a general housekeeper.

Emily did not mind the workload, for wasn't she now truly bettering herself? And she had savings too, a great accomplishment for so young a girl. A few more years, and she'd be able to pay her way through a teachers' training college. Now, with the Austro-Hungarian monarchy gone (which had by no means affected the tile business) and the Czechoslovak Republic well under way, young single women were being given ever so much more of a chance to become teachers, or librarians. . . .

Alas, young Emily had read too many romantic novels, usually out loud to her mistress suffering in bed. So, when some three years later a new and handsome gardener was employed to replace the old, ailing one, she was inclined to believe that such a fine young man must have been struck down by some sad misfortune and forced to earn his living by gardening – the more so as it soon became apparent that he was not very good at it. And when he started serenading her, standing there amidst wilting vegetables under the kitchen window and singing up to her little attic which was just two storeys above the kitchen, her heart was singing too.

In a year and a half, when their employers decided to move to Vienna and could bear to part with Emily, she and Václav the gardener were duly wed. The winter was cruel that year and there was so much snow that only the horses' ears could be seen over the snow-hedges as they drove the open carriage with the newly-weds through narrow cleared passages on the country lanes. And although the priest's housekeeper had placed red-hot bricks under their feet and thrust a burning potato into each of their hands, they arrived in Emily's village half frozen, and it took plenty of the rich uncle's *slivovic* to revive them. The *slivovic* was sent as a clear recognition that Emily was on her way up in the world.

In less than ten years, however, Emily and Václav had come to Prague with only their two children for possessions, to join the proletariat. Emily's mouth was set in a thin, bitter line and she hid her small hands, which had become claw-like through toil with soil and roots, in cheap cotton gloves. And Václav, as handsome as ever apart from rotting teeth, appeared muted and not quite to understand what had happened; he struck his new neighbours as being gentle and half-witted as an ox; he never went with the other fellows for a drink; he was also rumoured to be impotent.

The inevitable had happened. Václav was no Prince Charming. An only child of a retired soldier and a tall farm-maid (the first Czech maiden his father had met as he hopped back across half of Europe on his one leg and a crutch, and brought to his home village), Václav was a broken lad very early. The family lived in a dwelling which had a brick front, but the rest of it was a sandstone cave. He went to school for two winters only, and was glad to get rid of it for he was mercilessly bullied for being slow and born out of wedlock and the village's poor. His mother beat him a lot, unhappy as she was, and if his father tried to stop her, she beat him too, with his own crutch.

For some reason or other, Václav desperately wanted to be a tailor, though he was bulky and tall and quite strong. But to be sent to town to learn that particular profession, any profession, cost money, and money was something his parents never saw – they worked for scraps of food and old clothing. He was sent to the castle instead and became a kitchen boy, and when he'd outgrown that, a gardener's boy. He was gentle and obedient but constantly frightened, by the horses and the hounds and the governesses and the old gardener himself. Thus he never learned anything properly, and lost all ambition.

The old duchess gone with the old monarchy, and the castle nationalized, Václav had nowhere to go; he moved from town to town around Bohemia doing odd jobs, growing rather handsome and looking bold, although his blue eyes retained the gentleness which was really fear. He approached Emily's mistress in the market – pure luck, for she only went once a month, when it was a laundry day for poor Emily – and brought her dainty baskets back to the villa. Overwhelmed, really quite touched, the *gnädige Frau* had employed him on the spot.

*

28

With Emily's savings, Václav paid the lease on their first vegetable garden and the little cottage that went with it. But it was in a region where there were too many people in the same business, so the markets were overflowing with vegetables and prices were dropping. Only the most efficient and the most versatile could hope for success; Václav was neither, not even with Emily toiling harder than any of their seasonal helpers, and taking over all the paperwork. They had to give up, and with a little daughter on their hands they moved to a smaller garden and a smaller cottage which Emily had chosen. At last they were doing all right; they had a few happy years and a son. Emily had become the boss, and Václav wouldn't have minded really, if only the chaps in the pub hadn't nagged him so much. He was never a drinking man, but it was a matter of status to go to the pub on Saturdays and Emily encouraged him to do so, giving him just the right amount of money to spend. But the chaps kept sneering at him. . . .

One winter's day just before Christmas, when Emily and the children were away visiting Emily's parents and unmarried sisters, Václav discovered an advertisement in the agricultural magazine which Emily subscribed to, and took a deep breath. Here was a bargain! Acres of well-established vegetable beds, an apple orchard and a rose garden. Emily would love that! For practically nothing – well, for just about as much as they had stored away in the National Savings Bank. He would show her that he had initiative, that he had ambition!

A Prague telephone number was given; Václav went to the post office without even putting his coat on, strolled happily through the sleet and startled the postmaster. With considerable effort and confusion, he made the first long-distance call of his life.

Next day a man in a rather showy fur coat arrived, congratulated Václav on his decision, drove him to the bank and back in his motor car and crisply finished the business by exchanging some impressive-looking papers with lots of stamps for Václav's money. The man gone, Václav felt as though he had single-handedly performed a miracle.

Emily cried and cried when he told her; strange woman.

The following morning, she left the children with their nearest neighbour and marched Václav two miles to the railway station. It took them three hours on the train and an hour more on a bus to reach the place in south-west Bohemia where the property should have been, and all that time Emily was silently praying. But of course there was no garden, no rosebeds, no orchard, no house; nothing, just acres of an old snow-covered cemetery. People in the small hamlet shook their heads at them, without understanding, without pity. The Prague telephone number proved to be the number of a busy café-restaurant; the proprietor and the police merely shrugged their shoulders.

Emily withdrew all her warmth from Václav; turned into a stone. She sold what she could to pay the outstanding lease on their place, although the owner wouldn't have insisted; but pride was something Emily could not do without. With her heart bleeding and her face dead, Emily moved the family to Prague, where an unmarried cousin living in sin with a married man offered temporary shelter.

From week one, Emily slaved twelve hours a day scrubbing floors in hospitals and schools; for Václav, there was little else to do apart from shovelling snow and unloading coal wagons, and perhaps some cabbage-picking in summer in the fields around Prague. She took every penny from him, and after one savage year she had enough to rent a small grocery shop, which went with one-room basement accommodation in a pleasant suburb near the Tree Park, the biggest park in Prague.

In the same year, Prague was occupied by Nazi Germany. Mercilessly, Emily forced her bewildered husband to take one of the jobs the Germans were offering; he became a second gardener in a vegetable garden catering for an SS officers' mess. He shivered and sweated at the mere sight of a Nazi uniform but the money wasn't too bad, and at last Václav felt, after two years, a bit of a man.

One day in June he was given the afternoon off and came home just when Emily had closed the shop during the lunch hour and was resting in bed, her feet on the pillows. He lay down beside her and she did not protest; she felt warmer towards him, now that she had her shop and was on her way up again; and anyway he was impotent, poor soul, she had come to terms with that, she was almost glad of it as they had to share the double bed with the children; unsuspecting, she let him caress her.

She gave such a sharp angry cry and was so hostile afterwards that Václav's potency vanished forever, at the age of forty. He had, however, made Emily pregnant, and the baby was due in February.

Emily tried to get an abortion but didn't know where to turn. She paid a large sum of money for some pills that did not work and finally, her belly high and heavy and her soul in cold agony, she closed the shop, negotiated to keep the basement flat and gave up the hope of bettering herself forever.

Hela, the daughter, was twelve years old and the boy, Jan, was eight when Linda was born. They were both fine children, with brown eyes and dark hair just like their mother's, from whom they had taken their brains too. They did not mind having a little sister and Emily's heart warmed to them even more, because she knew, she *knew* that she would never be able to love the child. And it was as if the baby had known it: there was, in its black-blue eyes, a look that was fiercely independent.

For her elder children Emily now had plans. They would achieve everything she had ever wanted, and more. The road to such heights leads through education; they would go to school; she would scrub floors again to keep them there.

The little savage will have to find her way in life without my support, thought Emily, she'll have men helping her along; look at the way her father dotes on her, and the doctor when he comes, always crooning over her. And sometimes, when she looked at the growing golden-haired child, Emily had to fight back an ugly thought: maybe it isn't my child at all. The other two were born at home, in her own bed; this one was born in a big, busy hospital – anything could have happened there. . . .

She takes, however, good care of the child, as a conscientious foster parent would. And she keeps the home spotless, cooks the meals, does the laundry – her washing line always greatly admired – irons her husband's shirts, darns his socks and keeps him from making too big a fool of himself, and slaves around to earn money. Suffering, as she is to discover later, from tuberculosis, which she now takes for mere fatigue.

Poor proud Emily.

Dear John,

Before I say anything else, I want you to know how good it is to walk across the meadow and through the bog to the stream, fill the buckets with water and trudge back, with the idea of you at my side. I like my strength, and I think I would resent it if you tried to carry the buckets for me; but of course you don't. You like my strength too.

About Poor Emily: I gathered bits and pieces of her story as I grew up, but of course the basic ones were missing. I knew she didn't want me and tried to have me 'scrubbed-out' before I was even born; Mrs Pokorná/Humble threw that bit – with fairly elaborate details – at me, when she caught me being naughty to her ballet-going, piano-playing daughter. I believe I was, too, because I took it as a fair revenge; it was only after I told my mother, wanting her to laugh it off and she, in her merciless honesty, quietly confirmed it, that the blow struck. It still didn't necessarily mean that she did not love me *after* I was born, but the harm was done: I began to look for love, and found none.

Between five and six years of age, during each illness – I was catching every one on the children's doctor's list – I watched for signs: she bathed me and fed me, she stayed up at night to give me medicine, smooth my pillow and wet my lips, but behind the worry in her eyes there was an unbroken pool of indifference. So, one day, I asked.

'Every mother is fond of her children,' she said and turned away, without even pretending a kiss or a pat on the cheek.

I only wish she had told me why she couldn't love me much earlier than she finally did; I needn't have grown up believing I was too ugly to be loved.

She told me the whole story when my daughter was born,

much too late for me and for herself, but in the nick of time for my daughter – I could have repeated the pattern! For the first time in my life, I was allowed to kiss my mother on the cheek. It was old and withered and velvety, like an apple in winter, but she blushed like a maiden. Dear John, there was murder in my heart! – but I did not let her know.

How she loved my daughter! Passionately, kindly, humorously, never missing a trick or treat, for six long years. Until the day when her heart gave a leap and she groped for bed, stretched out, smiled an apology and died.

Don't you believe she went to her grave! She went straight into my dreams, she had no difficulty finding an entrance. Since then, it has been a tug-of-war, with mother winning. Some dreams she had all for herself, but listen: with all her blushing and maidenhood, my mother did not shrink from entering some of my wildest erotic dreams. By and by, she forced me to stop having them; until, at the age of forty, I made – inevitably and in my waking hours – a decision that sex is an undignified burden for an intelligent woman.

Did I tell you that I actually developed all the pains and aches she suffered from, without having the disease that caused them?

Dearest John, is all this too dreary for you? No, I know it isn't; (a) you must feel that I am winning now, and (b) I too am catching a glimpse of some fundamental kindness behind all this.

The sun was pink and sleepy when I began this letter, dear John. Now the night is dark and my fire but a dull glow, and I am sleepy too. There is a taste of happiness on the tip of my tongue and a feather-touch of freedom upon my brow. I shall rise at dawn: I cannot wait to follow it and write it down for you.

Sleep well, my pleasure, sleep well.

L.

Little Linda

Every other afternoon, come summer, come winter, there is a child in the Tree Park, the biggest park in Prague, which shouldn't have been there on its own. Not that the world

33

cares much at the moment, the world is at war and thousands of children are dying from bullets, from bombs ... from gas.

This particular child doesn't care about the world either; it runs like a squirrel from tree to tree, hiding among them all, though there is one tree it loves most of all. It's a large old oak tree with its roots arched above the ground so that they look like the thighs, knees and calves of a five-legged giant comfortably seated on the grass with legs apart. There the child settles down to play with its jasmine-bud midgets, poppy-queens and twig-people, to make up and sing Big songs and Small songs and Sad ones and Bad ones.

At the first sign of darkness, the child runs home, having already mastered the law of freedom: the longer one wants to keep it, the more one must observe its outer limits.

At the gate, she – for little Linda it is – makes herself invisible, by magic even she could not explain; she must never be caught actually leaving the Tree Park, which is strictly out of bounds for unaccompanied little brats. Only when deep in her street does she make herself visible again to her brother and sister and their friends; then they take their time to see her, for they are enjoying some of their own forbidden games under the cover of a search party.

In the end, they all march home and the neighbourhood can slowly go to bed.

But of course there are days and *days*.

Day. It is hot, hotter, hottest. Linda can tell by the whimpering of babies on the promenade above and the puffing noises their mothers make; by the thirsty little songs and short flights of birds; by the frenzy and the buzz of flies. Her poppy-queens wilt in her hands and she has to bury them while making up a funeral song; the earth is full of bugs and beetles cooling themselves.

The funeral song is turning out grand and Linda is singing it out loud, which is all right, for she can tell by her back-ears that all the mothers and babies have gone. Which is strange.

The light is also strange. There is a hugeness in the air,

a gigantic silence; nobody is buzzing or singing any more, nothing moves. Linda runs onto a path where she can see: there is no sun, the sky is split; one half has no colour at all, the other, the cloud, is yellow. A sickly smell is rising, it comes from the limp, sweaty, motionless leaves, it clutches at Linda's stomach; she wants to run home, only she can't, she can't wiggle a toe.

And there *it comes*. A huge yellow leg shoots down from the sky and stamps the ground, it yells and howls and whirls towards her, it whips and it burns. Only now is the spell broken and Linda can run to her oak tree; she crawls under the nearest arched knee of the root, burying herself as deep as she can.

And there is Crashing, Breaking, Swishing. But the sickly smell is gone; Linda knows the word for it now, it's a word she often marvelled at and did not know the proper meaning of: fear. There is a different smell in the air, and Linda has a word for it too, it is power, it is rather wonderful and she sings a powerful song. Only it is getting too wonderful and Linda knows that she must sleep a little now, or else she will burst.

And so she sleeps a little and wakes up when all is peaceful again. It rains, but the large drops are few and wide apart, they fall to the ground covered in dust and roll about like those silvery balls from a broken thermometer.

Little Linda works her way home now and it is difficult, there are large holes in the earth and dead trees and branches lying on the ground. Linda can tell that this is serious, and prepares to make herself double-invisible at the gate.

Maybe she will even have to tell a lie.

Day. Mother is wearing a hat and that means she is also holding Linda's hand firmly and talking to a woman who always comes with a child Linda hates. Soon they will be supposed to play and the stupid thing will cry whatever Linda does. But the woman and the child do not come often and it's worth waiting for mother to say the curious words Linda takes such a strange delight in.

'They must have swopped the babies in the maternity

ward! This child cannot be mine! She is a gypsy, she must have been brought in from a tinkers' wagon! One of these days, I'll send her back!'

Upon which they all prepare to leave the Tree Park, only Linda makes herself vanish, and stays behind, to sing a gypsy song.

Day. Linda is kneeling in soft fresh snow, white, whiter, whitest. By opening her arms wide and then slowly closing them again, she can gather a mountain of snow; worked upon, it will provide a beautiful, noble castle for her twig-people.

Something dark and shivering lies on the grass where Linda's arm shovelled the snow away: a little bird! Linda picks it up in her gloved hands, but that won't do, they must be ice-cold; she slips out of her gloves and hugs the bird between her warm hands and blows as much hot breath at it as she can muster. The shiny yellow beak opens and shuts again; one tiny eye looks at Linda in agony and then gets slowly covered by a horrible lid of Death; the small body gives a shudder and the lovely red feet stretch out in rigidity.

There is not a song about this, not yet. Hot gushes of grief form in the pit of Linda's stomach, they mount and flood her heart and her mouth, her nose and her eyes. She drops the bird and runs to her oak tree and sheds her burning tears on its dear old rough skin, they flow and flow until none are left and a real funeral song sits all salty and warm on her tongue.

But when she turns back to her snow mountain, there is no bird on top of it. A large black crow is stealing it away, half hopping and half flying, flapping its wings noisily and tossing the tiny body in its powerful beak as if it wanted to kill it once again.

'Death!' Linda screams at the crow. 'You Double-Death!' And she is sick, and she runs home, to get a Fever and a Lemonade and a Fever again.

As the world war nears its end, more and more *days* happen

outside the Tree Park, too. In fact, they'd better: what with the air raids on and the strange voices on the radio, Emily hardly ever goes out to work, she takes other people's laundry in instead; there aren't many chances for little Linda to escape.

Day. Father is saying '*Jawohl!*' to a pair of shiny boots in a strange squeaky voice, not his usual warm and silly one. A hand belongs to the boots and now it is placed on Linda's head, it is cool and dry and quite pleasant, but Linda won't lift her eyes. Not on her life! She is looking at a fat green caterpillar with yellow dots and black fur and a million hairy legs working its way across a fat green cucumber with yellow streaks.

Day. Under a massive table in a corner of the coal cellar-cum-bomb shelter, little Linda is looking after a baby in its basket. There isn't much to do for the baby is asleep, but it gives her a good excuse to stay away from the tense, shifting bodies sitting on the table and all around and smelling of fear.

And she can, undisturbed and as slowly as she likes, savour the first doughnut in her life: yummy, yummier, yummiest. It is a present from the landlady; something must have moved her cold, avaricious, child-hating heart.

There is a thunder and a shudder, only it is not coming from above, it is coming from under and it heaves the ground, slightly but unmistakably. The baby smacks its lips and sleeps on; Linda does the same and goes on nibbling; but a tiny grey mouse, in great distress, comes out of her hole and runs up Linda's skirts onto her lap.

The powerful smell of the doughnut makes the mouse forget her fears; it works wonders with little Linda too. She takes another measured mouth-watering bite and slowly, slowly, puts her hand with the doughnut down on her lap, an inch from the excited tail-wagging and sniffing creature. And oh, cross my heart, the mouse doesn't run away; with the funniest speedy movements of its tiniest teeth and mouth and head, it saws off quite a sizeable bit of the doughnut and starts munching it right there, on little Linda's lap.

For a while, the mouse and the child have a lovely time together. Not even the second thunder-under would have disturbed them; 'Germans,' says Linda to the mouse and puts as much contempt into her voice as she can find in her mind.

'Americans, you silly billy,' says brother Jan and makes the mouse run away, as he squeezes his leggy body into what little space is left under the table.

'Americans' is a word which tells Linda nothing, but even when it does, it will remain forever associated with a heaving ground, a mouse, and a doughnut.

Day. The tanks make enough noise to send you crazy, but Linda isn't listening, she is looking. A mountain of people grew in the middle of the road! It's like an anthill really, only bigger and friendlier. On one side of the mountain there is a long nozzle and Linda's brother and his mates are sitting and swinging on it like a bunch of monkeys.

Linda is deciding whether to like this or not, she probably will, for the squirming mountain is adorned by dozens of bunches of pink, blue, purple, red and white lilac blossoms. An arm shoots out from the top of the heap, a strong brown arm with at least five wristwatches between its wrist and elbow, and it is holding a gun, pointed at the sky.

Linda can't help listening now, for the gun makes such sharp spluttering noises and all these people are laughing and crying and singing even more, and the pigeons are flying about in utter panic and nobody cares. *Ratatata* goes the gun again and a pigeon falls flat on the roof and rolls down and falls again, and another.

'Pigeons!' shouts little Linda. 'Pigeons!'

And she tugs at the nearest adult's shirt, it is Mr Beránek/Lamb; he gives another trill on his mouth organ and tussles Linda's hair.

'Russians, child! Russians, brothers, tanks and all!' he shouts merrily back. 'All will be well now!'

And he goes on with his squealy music and even does a

38

phoney tap dance; little Linda, however, starts piddijoeing, brushing her lower lip with her little finger, a soothing gesture of her babyhood which one would have thought she'd long forgotten.

Day. Linda keeps right on piddijoeing when nobody's watching; and nobody is, everybody's jumping about with the Russians. Everybody but the landlady who finds little Linda sulking by the back door, unlocks it and lets the child into her own private sanctuary, a clustered bit of a backyard with a pitifully neglected bed of roses.

Now Linda is really worried; she applies her little finger with such speed that it hurts. Don't all children know that the landlady is a wicked witch?! And here she is coming back, surely to chop Linda up and eat her! That's why she gave her the blasted doughnut, to make her fatter!

But the landlady is holding a strange, beautiful rag doll with a sheer wonder of a painted china head; not even Mrs Pokorná/Humble has such in store for her goose of a daughter.

'You don't like the Russians either, do you, child? I can see that nitwit of your father becoming a communist; you poor thing! God knows what will happen to decent people with a bit of property! Do you know what's going on in the Tree Park? They chop down trees to make fires, they eat all the ducks and swans and squirrels, even crows, God help us!'

Breathing heavily, the old woman starts fiddling with her sickly roses, leaving the doll in little Linda's care. But for one reason or other, Linda is no longer bewitched by the long-legged, staring, lace-clad and moth-smelling creature; she holds it politely and carefully in her lap, seated on an equally antiquated stool with only three legs to it.

'So the Russians eat crows, hey?' she whispers towards the doll's delicately curved ears. 'Well let me tell you, crows are the wickedest! The Russians must be good soldiers, very hungry, and very, very brave!' Having reached this conclusion, Linda no longer thinks of piddijoeing, and she throws the doll in the air.

But the stupid doll can't take it, it is a witch's creature all right. There is a flash, a terrific bang, a nasty squealing sound – and the doll's china head bursts into a thousand white splinters, the beheaded body flying too far away for Linda to catch. Linda's lip is cut by a splinter, and so is her arm, and the doll is clearly beyond repair, but it seems to have nothing to do with the horrible, everlasting scream coming out of the landlady's gaping mouth, black against her bleached face.

There is a great deal of fuss for the rest of the day, everybody treating Linda to sweets, praising the Russians and cursing the German soldier who was holding out in the attic above the café until he had to be blasted dead with a grenade.

That night, sleep comes slowly to little Linda, so she treats her lower lip to its last brush of piddijoeing ever.

Day. '*Dotchka, dotchka,*' cries the big old Russian, leaning out of the Jeep and picking Linda up.

'*Dotchka, dotchka,*' it is for most of the ride, and lots of scratchy kisses by a sharp-smelling mouth. The young one at the wheel, the one without hair and with only one ear, keeps laughing all the way down the hill and up again through narrow streets to the beautifulest square Linda's ever seen, fit for queens and kings.

She is left alone in the Jeep, holding a silvery something, which the big old one pressed into her hand.

'*Shokolat,*' he said, '*Hollandskyi.*'

It seems to get softer in her hand. Surely, it cannot be wrong to look what's happening to it, the soldier must want her to take good care of it. The silver wrapping undone, the brown squares with softened edges give out such a rich, sweet smell, bitter and warm all at once, that Linda just has to give it a lick. And it is out of this world, it's queens and kings, it's tasty, tastier, tastiest, it's utterly and absolutely overwhelming.

'*Shokolat,*' sighs Linda happily, '*Hollandskyi.*'

And she eats the whole thing, here and now, and licks the wrapping clean. And she knows she must sleep a little, or rather a lot, for this thing cannot be anything else but the sweet sin people talk about!

Much later, there is a great deal of fuss all right, but Linda is holding onto her sleep, just listening a bit. Her sticky mouth and fingers are washed and she is being undressed and lowered into her pram; will they never buy her a bed? Now that she has sinned?

Neighbours keep coming in and out and everybody wants to hear the story about little Linda having been kidnapped by the Russians and missing till late at night. But apparently they did no harm apart from stuffing the child with chocolate. The young driver fortunately remembered the street where they'd picked her up and brought her home. As far as Mr Hrdlička/Dove who speaks a bit of Russian could understand, it appears that the old sergeant left a child just like Linda far back in Russia when he went to war. War had made him a little crazy in the head, and victory even more, and he snatched little Linda thinking it was his own daughter. That's what '*dotchka*' meant, the good neighbour explained.

'*Dotchka*, my foot,' Linda thinks, losing interest and preparing for a big sleep, still deliciously stuffed with rich mellow sweetness. '*Shokolat, Hollandskyi!*'

Day. A slow procession of silent, limping men in bandages and torn uniforms is moving down the High Street.

'Germans!' little Linda wants to say with contempt but, because of a strange lump in her throat, she can't.

Russian soldiers march on both sides of the procession, their guns pointing low, their faces solemn. The butcher from the High Street market, wearing a red badge on his sleeve and snapping a horse whip in each hand, does most of the shouting, echoed by the crowds. The man with his red face and enormous hands has always been a terror to little Linda; she bites her lip.

'*Los, los*, you murdering swines,' roars the butcher, '*Los*, you bloodsuckers, you motherfuckers, you pig's hairs, you rotting German mincemeat!'

His whip carves a quickly bleeding line across a German's face, and for a moment the crowds go silent.

'You shit of a butcher,' Linda says in a clear carrying voice, and brother Jan hurries her out of the crowd and home.

Day. Linda's been in a church before, but then it was always full of coughing people, never empty and quiet and dark like this one is. Linda's found it by following the outline of the Tree Park outside its walls, the first venture of this kind.

Linda is frowning, deeply bothered; she can tell that her heart is open wide, by the ice-cold streams that are flowing through it. She wanders around stepping as lightly as she can, touching the polished wooden toes of the Holy People.

A shaft of sun penetrates the colourful window and it is as if fear and power came to be one with beauty. It makes little Linda spin around, raise her arms and sing a song, her best ever.

'Oh Holy Rainbow, Oh Holy Eye of Eye! Oh Holy Tree, Oh Shokolat, Oh Holy Leg of Sky!'

An iron hand grips her ear and pulls and drags her to the door and out.

'Out with you, you miserable child! You little pagan, you!'

Little Linda lies in wait for brother Jan to come out of school.

'Am I a pagan?' she asks anxiously, but he only scowls at her and runs off with his mates. In the evening, however, when they are all playing on the street, he finds a moment.

'Mother says you've been baptized all right, but that you're a complete mystery of a child and a pagan at heart. Beats me!' he concludes and off he runs again.

Linda makes herself invisible and marvels at the word 'mystery' and finds it to be the best of all words so far.

Day. Linda is sitting on her father's knee listening to a long sad story about the time when he was a gardener's boy in a castle which stood in the middle of a huge park where a duchess roamed on horseback frightening him to death.

'Was I there?' she asks, thrilled by the vision.

'You certainly were not,' laughs father.

'Where was I then?'

Father looks teasingly at mother but she will not smile.

'You were still picking mushrooms, that's where you were!' says father and pinches Linda's cheek. Linda sighs with happiness. It means that she was there all the time, even unborn, sleeping on soft silvery moss, jumping through friendly warm woods with little creatures, picking wild mushrooms, waiting without haste for the gypsies to come along, or mother.

Many days are passing between *days* and little Linda is quickly growing into another age in which she is going to be the best pupil in the whole school, a winner of all the prizes, a Red Pioneer and a girl so ugly that she cannot be loved by her own mother.

John,

Sorry to bother you so late at night, but this is a cry for help. I am cold and shivering, and it is not merely because the weather has changed, although the last sunset, before the clouds took over, was pretty scary. None of the usual pink-scarlet wonder; red pool of blood spilled over half a sky. No wind blew where I stood watching; yet black rugged clouds rose from behind the mountains and darted over the bleeding sky like Harpies. The fury is in the rain, too; swishing downpour beating the grass into the ground; I can feel the slender necks of daffodils snapping one by one.

Something else has happened to me; while I was spending happy days over little Linda, I could not sleep at night. This is the fifth night I've stayed awake, listening to the sound.

It is a peculiar, persistent humming in two very deep and vibrant tones, changing from one to another at irregular intervals. It sounds like some devil at work deep in the mountain, like some sinister engineering device boring into the rocks, reaching towards the soft centre of the Earth. At first I believed that that's what it must be, I actually thought

43

of walking down to the village in the morning to tell people about it, to warn them. It was making me dizzy; trying to stop it, I covered my ears with my hands as tight as I could.

And there it was, John, ten times louder!

It's all in my head, the vibrant chord is strung between my ears. By all this searching and remembering, I must have stumbled upon some vital veins and caused a short, and now I am listening in on my bloodstream, on all the microscopic living and rotting that goes on in my body.

Or it's a devil's work all right, some carnivorous devil who is holding my body together in its skin bag, waiting for the billions of creepy little cells to become ripe for slaughter. Humming into my ears, he wants me to know that life is not measured by light years, that it is not a transparent medium in which I could travel back and forth with little danger; death years are the true measure and trying to work against their current, he lets me know, I am wading in rot which must – at my age – be waist-deep.

What am I doing, waving sheets of paper scribbled over with imaginary you and imaginary I, with words carefully washed of all dirt, in the devil's face? Shoo shoo, naughty devil, why don't you put some clothes on?!

Hadn't even little Linda known better when she contracted child-worms and her mother made her look at her shit? The tiny white squirming things had travelled up her little cunt, and mother made her look at it too, to break her resistance to the potent garlic soup cure. The neat worms weren't scary; the horror was to discover that there is rot inside her, inside all living things, not just the dead. And that there is a soft, creepy pleasure in smelling it! However strongly your mind denies it. . . .

Please help me, John, help me go on denying it! I don't stand a chance in life if I cannot shelter in the mind, my mind, your mind! I've had my share of hearty physical living. Ben Strizlik, my husband, was a champion of it and not over-sensitive to signals of distress; but even he knew I was pretending. I suppose I am one of nature's mishaps; a social misfit; a pagan. I don't believe in God, but I do, I do believe in creation! I have created you, out of remembered shapes and pure desires. You shall not die. You exist as I

44

wish to exist. If you stay with me through all this ordering and straightening out of my past, of the visions of it, I believe I shall build a castle for you and me, an indestructible home.

I know you can't make the devil's humming stop! All I ask is – don't fade away. I have not tied you to a particular place; live in whatever wilderness, whatever bustling city you wish, but, please, stay within reach!

Please, John.

L.

Dearest John,

The morning is bright and breezy, little rains come from nowhere and the sun is laughing. I have surprised you by the stream among cowslips, violets and buttercups, chasing a shadow of a dipper. Thanks.

I can do without sleep, but not without you.

I love you John, my lamb, my shepherd, my wisdom tooth, my peace of mind; I love you.

L.

PS Please don't worry, I exist very well on canned food, crispbread and lots of onions. I have a bulb of garlic, too; I think I may go on the garlic soup cure; just to be on the safe side.

Joseph Stalin

Between her seventh and twelfth years Linda Střízlík/Wren was in love with Joseph Stalin. She came to love him through the art of socialist realism, not so much poetry and sculpture as cinema and painting; and through the overwhelming knowledge that he, Joseph Stalin, loved her.

Her teacher, an emotional lady with bleached hair, had told her so, and her mother, when asked, confirmed it with a dark remark, eyeing her skinny child with the usual suspicion:

'I wouldn't put it past you!' This added a touch of mystery to the love affair.

Emily herself found no reason why she should love Joseph Stalin; she had come to distrust men in general and handsome men in particular. Apart, of course, from her son Jan; her love for the boy was excruciating. Jan often thought her rather abrupt; he did not know that when she cut him short and left him, it was to hide tears of overflowing emotion.

Emily was a practical woman and she knew that what Joseph Stalin once won, he would not give away, and there were enough rumours about the darker sides of his power to make him a rather undesirable Father for the Nation. On the other hand, for the same practical reasons, Emily had little to say against communism. It held no threat against her and her family and even though it promised no riches either, especially if one had such a weak gentle soul for a husband, it had two distinct advantages.

First, she no longer had to slave for her children's future. The state would pay to have them educated, almost bribe them with all kinds of grants; any school would be overjoyed to have them, even if they weren't all that brilliant. They were the children of the working class, the hitherto under-privileged, who from now on were to have their way up paved broad and smooth whether they wanted it or not. As far as Emily was concerned, there was an undeniable justice in it, whatever some people might say.

She wouldn't, however, rely on justice alone; she saw to it that her children had a bonus: their undoubtedly proletarian father was a communist too. Václav Střízlík/Wren, with his wife's strong encouragement, had become a member of the communist party in 1945. He never made a career of it, it was pick and shovel for the rest of his life, but his children profited mildly.

Secondly, with all medical care free, she no longer had to pretend that she was merely tired. She was sent to what used to be a first-class, really quite posh, sanatorium, and even though it rapidly deteriorated to second-class and below, and was rather crowded, Emily still enjoyed her leisure. Doctors and nurses were very fond of this cheerful, smiling, uncomplaining woman, whose tuberculosis was badly advanced and painful.

Upon her return, and before she had to undergo another prolonged cure, Emily took on voluntary work for the local branch of the Socialist Women's Union, gaining respect for bringing some decency into that quarrelsome body of over-excitable, flag-waving and anxious women. It was her idea, amongst others, to replace the portrait of Joseph Stalin looming over the meeting room-cum-office with that of La Passionaria, whose stern face had a decidedly calming effect.

Only after Emily's death had it become known that throughout the twenty-five years she lived in socialism, she had secretly kept all members of her family on the Evangelical church list, paying the annual contributions out of her meagre savings. Whether out of kindness to the persecuted church or out of a desire to play it safe with her Maker is anybody's guess.

In the evenings, when the family gathered around the new kitchen table to dine on their potato goulash or dumplings with dill sauce or pancakes or sweet dumplings or carrot stew (meat remained a Sunday treat for which Emily had to queue four hours each Saturday), Emily would tolerate no politics.

She had a very good reason; Václav Střízlík/Wren, who had become a second gardener in the Tree Park, had developed a very peculiar political theory indeed. The older children would have either laughed at him or quarrelled with him, neither of which was permissible in a good family; and there was always the danger that little Linda might repeat some of it in school, which wouldn't do at all. Only after Hela and Jan ran off to their evening classes or youth clubs and Linda was in bed in the other room would Emily, safely anchored by her knitting or darning or sewing, listen to Václav's querulous musings.

Václav enjoyed these evenings in the family's new two-room flat very much, although the flat itself was in fact another of his failures. During the first days after the war, he was dispatched by Emily to talk to the local National Liberation Committee and claim one of those empty apartments the Germans had left behind. Since his family's living conditions were about the worst in the whole neighbourhood and he had a fresh communist party card in his pocket, Václav ought to have stood a good chance. Several times he went, and always came home empty-handed, while Mr Beránek/Lamb, for example, secured a four-bedroomed apartment full of mahogany furniture and silver cutlery. But, to Václav's surprise, Emily was not bitter. He could even tell that she was secretly pleased. Emily was ambitious but not greedy and certainly not immoral. She knew she could not have enjoyed living in one of those apartments which the Germans had most probably taken over from Jewish families, who had either fled when there was still time or had been herded into cattle wagons and never seen again.

Within a few months, she had found these two fourth-floor rooms full of light and with lots of sky behind their windows, only a few hundred yards from their basement, in Little Quick Street. There was no bathroom and no central heating, but there was the luxury of a completely private loo and a neat little larder into the bargain. So now they had a large kitchen-cum-living room with a couch for the boy to sleep on, and an even larger bedroom which they quickly got to call The Room. The parents, the child Linda and the grown-up girl Hela slept there. Come Christmas, the tree would be put up by the window, the ceiling-high, green-tiled stove would be lit for three days and nights, and the family would gather around. Otherwise only Jan would be permitted to use The Room during ordinary days, to practise his violin, and on Saturdays Hela would be allowed to serve coffee and cakes to her current fiancé there.

Linda went to bed willingly; she had waited for a proper bed of her own long enough, but she would never go straight to sleep, for that would be wasting a good thing. Before the great discovery of *Books*, Linda would sing quietly to herself, or listen to her father's voice coming only slightly muffled through the ill-fitting door.

Václav's politics were a pretty bad mishmash. Weak and soft as he was, the man had collected and cherished every cruel idiocy of his century. Rich and poor there always were, and always would be. A poor man never stands a chance against a Jew. Hitler was a dirty swine but one thing had to be said for him: he knew what he was doing when he killed the Jews. (Here Emily would hiss at him, but he

48

would come up with what he thought was a trump.) Look at Joseph Stalin, he hates them too. Whatever is wrong with the communist government is because the Jews have penetrated it. And because there are still too many monkish priests and ministers at large. Religion is the opium of the people and churches should be shut down, all of them. (Here, Emily would whisper something but Václav would not be shaken.) Poor people like him did not know any better, they had been poisoned by the opium fumes, until the party had opened their eyes. The party is doing a good job, the trouble is that a poor and honest man never really stands a chance. There are too many people getting rich again, on party jobs. Scoundrels, intellectuals and Jews. And too many women are taking men's places. Women should stay at home, take care of their children and husbands. The party should know better than to give them jobs, and far too many hopes. (Here, Emily would say something sharp, and Václav would retreat.) One thing is for certain; there is no greater man alive than Joseph Stalin, never was and never will be. The capitalist hyenas in the West may bare their teeth as much as they want, Joseph Stalin will defeat them with his little finger. The trouble is, a poor man never really gets to him, to tell him, as comrade to comrade, his problems . . . how the rich cheat the poor . . . always and always. (Here, Emily would hush him and soothe him and send him to bed, almost as if he were a child, and Linda would close her eyes and go to sleep, with Joseph Stalin in her heart. Only later, in her teens, would she remember the rest of her father's mumblings and cruelly, uncompromisingly hate him for them.)

Dear J.,

This is only a quick, undisciplined note, but I can't bring myself to wait with it. For a brief exercise, I ran up to the top of a steep rocky hill just behind the cottage, and saw a wren. Seeing it is nothing remarkable; a plain little bird. But hearing it! How can a bird so small have a voice so loud?! No fancy trills, just clear far-fetching notes of pure delight.

It cheered me up enormously: here is a cousin – however far removed – to look up to!

Wren, L.

There was a painting in the new wing of the National Gallery at the gate of Prague Castle, a monumental wonder in bright-coloured oil, covering an entire wall.

Generalissimus, said a golden plate underneath, but Linda would not be deceived. The man on top of the splendid marble staircase, godlike in his shining white uniform with gold trimmings, and handsome with his greying hair and bushy moustache, his penetrating eyes softened by a few lovable wrinkles smiling down at her, was Joseph Stalin and no other.

The sky was painted a warm, summery blue with a few darkish clouds evidently disappearing into the past. The marble pillars on each side of the staircase were adorned with vine leaves and hung with ripe dewy grapes. And on each stair, kneeling, sitting, standing, their faces and their arms raised in adoration towards the Generalissimus, were the lucky people painted to be with him forever: soldiers, workers, peasants, a man in a white coat who looked like a doctor, athletic young women and mellow-bodied mothers with children in their arms, a boy and a girl in Red Pioneer uniforms, an old man with a crutch. Flowers were scattered around and there was a large wreath made of golden wheat and barley with a few red poppies and blue cornflowers to make it merrier.

The gallery attendants soon got used to the skinny girl with two thin plaits of hair tied with white ribbons, who stood in front of the Stalin painting for long minutes at least twice a week; they thought she had probably been asked to study it for some school project, although, frankly, this was overdoing it a bit. Such an awful painting too; but this, of course, was not an opinion to be shared. Poor child.

Linda, her heart pounding, was imagining that she was the girl Pioneer in the painting, the one standing almost on the top of the staircase, holding out a bunch of red roses. Surely, in the next second beyond the painting's time, Joseph

Stalin would take it from her and give her a kiss or maybe lift her in his arms, as he often did in the movies.

But dreams are dreams; in reality, Linda stood no chance of being painted or kissed, she knew it only too well. She was smart enough, there was no other Pioneer in the whole city who could recite poems as well as she could, and she was always chosen to do recitations in the Castle, on state anniversaries and party birthdays, even for the President. But she was always coupled with Danda, a boy from her school, who stood beside her while she was doing the talking. It was he who was holding the bunch of roses, his cheeks even rosier than usual and his dimples deepening, his dark eyes round and large, a picture of a child as governments and parents like them, healthy and innocent. Invariably it was Danda who got the kiss and the embrace, while Linda stepped back and was forgotten but for some secretary who took down her name and school for future reference.

She did not mind; there were only two people in the whole world for whom she passionately wished to be kissworthy, her mother and Joseph Stalin. But with her ugliness, it would have taken a miracle, and miracles, under communism, did not happen.

Even without Joseph Stalin, Linda would probably have liked communism. It couldn't make her any prettier, nothing could, but it did give her dignity. There was no longer any shame in being poor, it had become – overnight, or so it seemed to her – an asset, a privilege, a pride. Maybe only for children, that was hard to tell; mother certainly treated Linda with more respect.

Linda knew all about indignity; she started school just a few months before communism, in 1947; at that time, parcels from America were still distributed around the country for the needy victims of war. One rainy day, the teacher asked all such children in her class who were 'socially weak' – well, in fact poor – to raise their hands. Linda did not, but the teacher put her name on the list nevertheless; in due time, the 'socially weak' children from all of Prague's schools were escorted to the town hall and sat in their hundreds in

51

row upon row of cold wooden seats. Speeches were made; and then, one by one, the children were called by name to the platform and received a large parcel each.

At home everybody was delighted; even proud Emily seemed to appreciate the tins of condensed milk and packets of cocoa and white flour. Sister Hela was beside herself about some silly faded jumpers and blouses, and brother Jan blushed with pleasure over a pair of old jeans.

The only piece of clothing which looked new was a bright red flannel dress with enormous green and yellow parrots printed on it, the most ridiculous thing anyone had ever seen. Linda howled with laughter, forgetting the indignities of the town hall; it was a joke, after all. Mother asked her to put it on, and Linda did, and danced a Red Indian war-dance in it, and laughed herself to hiccups . . . until she saw the look in her mother's eyes.

The skirt was shortened and the waist gathered in by mother's skilful fingers that very evening. Crying, pleading, choking with terror, Linda was made to wear the dress to school. The teacher sent a note, but Emily was not to be shaken; winter was coming and the dress was made of pure, warm, high-quality flannel. Only after brother Jan complained that his mates started calling him Parrot instead of Wren did Emily try to dye the parrots off. They proved totally resilient to such attempts and the dress was cut into leg-warming strips for father's gardening boots.

The episode took no more than two weeks; enough for the burning shame to leave scars in Linda's little soul forever – and to teach her about dignity.

Linda was twelve when Joseph Stalin died. She heard the news in town, where she was being X-rayed because of a suspected weak chest; travelling home on the open platform of tramway line number eight she cried her heart out. The clouds were white and swift on the winter sky and Linda's tear-flooded eyes transformed them into gigantic doves carrying Stalin's soul to Heaven and beyond. . . .

Everything pointed to an era of grief. Sister Hela was married but soon back home again, sitting up at nights by the window in the kitchen, smoking cigarettes and yelling at father whenever he feebly protested that the smoke was seeping into The Room through the ill-fitting door.

Brother Jan was serving his two years in the army, and when he came home on leave mother threw everybody out of the kitchen, bathed his blistered feet in a camilla-bath and endlessly whispered to him. From time to time, above her whisper, Linda could hear that Jan was sobbing; there was such despair in it and hatred and humiliation that her heart turned cold.

One morning Linda woke up with a heavy head and blue circles under her eyes and there was a bloodstain on her sheet. Mother sighed heavily, and for a moment she was compassionate and gentle. Then she presented Linda with the horrifying arsenal which those times, at least in that part of the world, had for menstruating women: a couple of home-crocheted crotchpieces with ribbons on each end which one tied to one's suspender belt, and a supply of rags cut out from old sheets. These had to be soaked in cold water, boiled, washed and dried for further use. It was a messy, smelly business, bewilderingly private and yet, on the washing line, terribly public; nothing but ache, shame and sorrow.

Life was never the same after Joseph Stalin died.

My dearest John,

The funny thing is that it never, not once, occurred to me to wish I was a man. I was going through awful times: big breasts grew on me while I was still skinny and shapeless; my hair turned a mousey colour, and greasy; I had spots and pimples all over my face and shoulders; I had panicky dreams about sweaty horses. Yet I developed considerable social skills: I was still the best in school but never swanky, I let anyone copy my schoolwork and my prompting was bold and efficient, I joined in every classroom mischief and stood up for the wrongly accused, and tried not to look hurt by being excluded from erotic games. Boys thought I was ugly, but straight and fun to be with. Girls admired my ability not to giggle and blush while addressing a hall full of pupils and teachers; little did they know that my knees were trembling and that I had to fight a dead faint whenever I had merely to enter a room with people in it. I was desperately unhappy, but I blamed it on something deeper than being a girl.

My ugliness was coming to the surface from the depth of my soul, which must have been contaminated, I felt, by some dark, uncanny touches of evil before I was born. I rediscovered solitary walks in the Tree Park, only I went much further than I used to as a child, all the way down to the river. There, on a small island by the rapids, if I concentrated hard enough, I could actually remember the turbulences and the spiralling whirlpool of my birth, and some glowing darkness that was catching up with me. . . .

And if you think, dear John, that all the books I devoured, anything I could lay my hands on from Dickens and Twain to Chekhov, Gorky and Romain Rolland, have helped me, don't. It was in all of them, that touch of unknown evil, that hereditary sorrow, thinly covered by the honey and wax of sweet, hopeful lies.

And there was something else in the books that was disturbing: men and women. It seemed all wrong. I could identify with neither of them. Men were . . . overbearing, intent on violence, even the weakest and gentlest among them were always grabbing, for eternity, for something. Women, apart from being beautiful (there, of course, I was jealous) or otherwise physical, were . . . short, limited; moral or immoral, deep or shallow, they were never reaching for anything but men.

Poetry was much better. After the age of fifteen, for a good couple of years, I stuck to it; I suppose I read almost every volume available in Czech. And I had a perfect place for reading poems: Stalin's left shoe.

The monstrous monument on the hill survived Stalin's death by seven years before it was dismantled. Its hundreds of tons of granite overlooked the winding river with its old bridges and the cluster of roofs and spires of the Old Town of Prague; the shoe itself was large enough to hide me from the passers-by below, yet it obstructed the beautiful view but little. An absolute place for a poetry-reading truant; I was no longer a believer, so there was no blasphemy.

My love, if ever I become a quiet Englishwoman on the outside and a free human being on the inside, it will be thanks to these nocturnal talks with you. I no longer write during the day; at dawn, I stand outside the *hafodty* watching rabbits hop by and birds waking up; in the mornings, I wander about the mountain or tread down to the mailbox; I sleep in the afternoons and wake before sunset, thus saving the nights for you, and never mind the devil.

Listen, I have never seen so many lambs in my life! I like them very much and pity them even more – for shall not these alert, beautiful creatures grow into fat bleating beasts? No, I am not being bitter, simply impatient with my old bleating self.

Goodness gracious, John, judging by the number of lambs and the cuckoo's callings, Easter must be just around the corner! Which means that the rightful owners of this paradise may soon arrive to spend a week or more! I don't mind terribly much, the cottage is big enough for me to keep my patterns without disturbing anybody, and I may enjoy company after two months of solitude *à deux*. I don't think they'll chase me out of here, after all I am looking after their property rather well. All I am afraid of is that you will be too shy to stay around: please, please stay, I promise not to embarrass you in any way in front of strangers!

Dearest, I know I am being ridiculous. I suppose I just love saying please to you.

It is a quiet dawn today. There is no wind and the daylight is seeping through pearl grey clouds which are once again touching the grass. Birds are lazy with their song and invisible, with the rest of the world. Your right hand is supporting my chin while your left hand is gently pressing against the small of my head, and I am purring with wellbeing.

L.

Brother Jan

There was always something about the boy which brought a lump to Emily's throat – a shyness, a genius . . . a doom. Oh, he was healthy enough, though he was small for his age as a child and never grew up tall. His feet were a slender shoe-size six, yet he kicked a good soccer ball and was not at all bad at cross-country running.

It was there when he withdrew into a corner, curved his lips as if he were smiling to himself and shut his eyes, the dark long eyelashes resting in shadowy half-moons upon his cheeks. It was there when he played the violin; and how he played it! Not a hesitant note, not a negligent stroke of the bow, not the tiniest screech of a string, not even at the beginning.

Not like Linda! When Jan outgrew the cheap, half-size violin Emily had bought, and his teacher gave him a magnificent old instrument, Emily wasn't going to waste a good thing. She passed the cardboard box, containing in its elongated pear-shape the small violin, the well-used bow and folded sheets of beginners' music, to Linda and sent her to the same old teacher.

But the child had failed pitifully; what a waste of money, what screeching, squealing sounds! Jan had laughed.

'Let her be, Mum! She's good with words, you'll see.'

Always out to defend the brat, maintaining that she was not a liar, that she was simply imagining things and shielding her little world as best she could; for his sake, Emily usually let Linda slip off the hook.

Jan went to a teachers' training college; he knew how much Emily wanted him to though she never said it in so many words. It was good for him, Emily kept reassuring herself, really the best. Music was part of the curriculum, yet he wasn't going to be a wandering Bohemian, he was going to be a teacher. She never missed a college concert – Jan was always a star. He played Khachaturian's *Sabre Dance* without any apparent effort, the fingers on his left hand dancing, his right arm bouncing up and down, his chin holding the violin firmly in place. Yet that wasn't the music he liked; at home, just for his mother's ears, he played slow, enchanted music, such as the Largo of Dvořák's *New World* Symphony.

He was doing well at the college, very well, and in all the right things, too. He was a vice-chairman of the communist youth organization and soon a candidate for party membership. Yet it was as if he were sleepwalking, or as if some small but vital part were missing in the engine that moved him.

It was not missing when he fell in love, but somehow Emily knew that that was not going to last. The girl had a dark, unapproachable beauty; she was taller than Jan and had high moral principles; Emily was guessing rightly when she thought that the girl was deeply, and secretly, religious. Her name was Frantishka but Jan had called her Fanny. Trust Hela to tease him about it: 'Fanny, little brother's Nanny!' until he truly and unexpectedly boxed her ears.

Hela cried in pain and fury but Emily did not come to her rescue. Hela had little business teasing Jan, she with her lame betrothals and broken marriages. What was wrong with that girl? Tall, well-built, really rather pretty, a successful professional woman, yet keen on housekeeping – and she couldn't keep a man!

Fanny vanished one day, left Prague without word or trace, and never wrote. Jan was silent, and did not touch the violin. The college was recruiting graduates for schools in the northern border regions of Bohemia, left desolate and open to all kinds of low elements from inland after the German population was forcibly expatriated a year after the war; Jan volunteered.

Emily knew that whatever other good or bad reasons he had, the fact that the compulsory conscription into the army was postponed for a year for such volunteers was of great importance to Jan. He dreaded the army.

That year, all seemed well with Jan. He wrote many cheerful letters from Ansdorf, he said he liked his pupils – half of them gypsies suffering from malnutrition and abuse – and he said he had found a girl, Jarka, whose father was a drunkard and who needed protection and love. Jarka wrote too, surprisingly childish letters for a woman of twenty.

And then the army took him and the nightmare began.

Each leave, Emily oiled and massaged his hands and nursed the bleeding blisters on his feet, but she could find no remedy for the torments of his soul. He wept and he raved in hoarse whispers, and most of the time Emily did not know what it was all about: the Big Swindle, the rule of stupidity, killer instincts made into ideology, dummies of class enemies to be ripped open with bayonets, teenage prostitutes hanging around the barracks, hollow-eyed political prisoners working in a uranium mine next to the shooting galleries, boozing officers and illiterate sergeants dealing in communism as if it were a porno market. . . .

All Emily could do was to whisper back, come on Jan dear, it's only two years, only another eighteen months, only another two hundred and eighty days, come on, you can do it, I've baked your favourite cake for you, we shall have a roast duck tomorrow, your aunt Anna has sent it, don't cry baby, don't say such awful things, don't think about it, hush my dear, hush.

Then, all of a sudden, Jan took special leave and married the girl Jarka in Ansdorf. Her drunken father and his new woman had thrown her out of the house, and a married teacher in a border region was immediately entitled to a nice home. They all went to the wedding, Emily, Václav, Hela and Linda; it was a jolly wedding and they all tiptoed through the half-empty house around the bedroom where Jan and Jarka were spending their three-day honeymoon. Emily was pleased: here was something for Jan to come back to, to hold on to.

And true enough, it worked like a charm. Jan spent his leaves with Jarka, exchanged poetic little letters with Linda, wrote postcards to the rest of the family, even made it to corporal. At the end of the summer of 1955 he was back in civvies and had to buy a whole new wardrobe, for even if he hadn't grown any taller he had certainly put on a lot of muscle. His face was sun-tanned and his eyes laughing. During the whole week he spent in Prague before going up to Ansdorf, he kept Emily blushing with happiness.

God knows she needed it. Her tuberculosis had surged up again and she was to go to a sanatorium-clinic in the mountains and probably undergo an operation; pneumothorax was the horrifying name doctors called it. She kept putting it off, but now she would go gladly, she would want to get well, why – there might be a grandchild soon, a dreamy little boy with long dark eyelashes. . . . Hela was back home once again, she'd keep house for Václav and Linda. There was nothing to worry about with Linda; she was going through some painful menstruations and frowned at her spots, but otherwise she was as bright and independent as ever, much too independent perhaps, but her teachers liked her; what more could one want?

Jan, however, knew better than that. He spent a long Sunday afternoon with Linda, and it was her turn to cry hot tears of doubt and shame. She had progressed to the high school level without giving it a thought, as if it was the most natural thing in the world for any child with some intelligence. The summer holidays over, she had not found her best friend Olga, a mathematical genius, in the classroom with her. Was she ill perhaps? Or had she gone to some better school without telling Linda? That wasn't like her; worried, Linda asked the form master. 'Was not admitted, I am afraid,' was the answer, the incredible answer with no sense in it; 'Did not fulfil conditions necessary for admission to higher education,' was the explanation. Olga, the genius?!

The first day of school over, Linda ran to the tiny apartment where Olga lived with her widowed mother. She found Olga in bed, the pillow soaked through by a continuous flood of tears. And she found out a whole lot more: the father was not dead, he was serving a twelve-year sentence in a labour camp, working in uranium mines between spells in prison hospitals. He had been convicted of treason five years ago, after he had given shelter for three days and nights to his cousin, a witness in the show trials with the party Jews, himself serving a life sentence while many of his 'fellow conspirators' had been executed.

'Father didn't do anything,' sobbed Olga, clutching Linda's hand. 'He just let him sleep on the couch and gave him some food!' But he was also half-Jewish and a general practitioner with a small private clientele; and now his only daughter, brighter than most, was to suffer.

'Why didn't you ever tell me?'

'Oh Linda, you wouldn't have had anything to do with me! You couldn't have been my friend, could you! You never knew anything, you never cared about what was happening to people, and I was sometimes furious with you, but most of the time I was glad, glad! Because I could keep you for a friend!'

That Sunday afternoon, Linda was twisting Jan's fingers around her own, pleading for innocence, asking about guilt, ready to hate Joseph Stalin and her own father, ready to leave school and go to work in a factory with Olga, ready to do anything but stand accused of privileges which were other people's tragedy.

But Jan had little comfort to offer.

'Just stay where you are, Linda, there are no easy exits. Everybody's on his own.'

Still, they browsed through the Tree Park hand in hand and it was good for Linda to know that they were in this together.

A fortnight before Christmas, Linda received a strangely urgent letter from Jan, asking her to come and stay with him and Jarka in Ansdorf, and be sure to make it before Christmas Eve. But Linda couldn't – or wouldn't – go: mother was very ill indeed, she had had her operation and was not recovering. Hela spent every weekend at her bedside, as father was no good with his whining and whimpering and children under sixteen were not admitted into the ward.

Those were strange weekends; father would sit in the kitchen listening to the wireless, his eyes red and blinking with tears that had become automatic. Against his feeble protests, Linda would curl up on the single armchair in the unheated Room, and read; they'd have silent, almost hostile meals together, warming up what Hela had cooked for them. Christmas would not be any different; Linda would have been aching to spend it with Jan – if it weren't for Jarka and her doll-like, silly prettiness. So she wrote a rather prim little letter to Jan and resigned herself to the drabness of life.

The telegram came on Christmas Eve, in the early afternoon. Hela was with mother, father hadn't come home from work yet, Linda was decorating the tree, humming an old little song that floated to the surface from the wilderness of her childhood.

Having paid the expectant postman a crown from the housekeeping money kept in a jar, Linda opened the telegram, rigid with fear. But it wasn't about mother. It read:

'Jan dead please come Jarka.'

For three years, Linda was unable to shed a tear or remember properly those five days spent in Ansdorf. Father had collapsed, mother was not to be told, not yet, not for months; Linda had travelled alone. Policemen found it strange to deal with a fifteen-year-old, but she behaved better than many adults – dry-eyed, silent, polite. She nodded when they demonstrated the gun Jan had shot himself with: an old rusty thing that just wouldn't work. Only it did, once; there was a small hole beneath Jan's left nipple and very little blood; he was killed instantly.

Jarka was bloated with tears and sweet cherry liquor, uncomprehending, incomprehensible. The school director was racked with guilt and sheepishly pleaded for absolution: a fortnight before Christmas, during a winter teachers' conference, Jan had passed him a note in which he had said he was going to shoot himself on Christmas Eve. He, the director, read it aloud and everyone at the round table had had a good laugh.

'You know how it is,' he said to Linda in a high-pitched voice.

'I know,' Linda nodded and the ice closed a full circle around her heart.

In his coffin, Jan was both unrecognizable and more himself than he had ever been. Linda kissed him and retired politely to make room for the undertakers and their hammers and nails. A violin was playing Dvořák's Largo and Linda was unobtrusively sick in her large, black-trimmed handkerchief, while Hela and father, who came up for the funeral, sobbed violently.

'You morbid little bitch,' Hela said afterwards, but she didn't mean it – or did she?

Emily came home four months later all dressed in black. While Václav wept and accused the unfaithful, frivolous Jarka for a thousandth time, Emily looked at Linda with eyes that knew. And Linda resented it, Linda wanted to shout 'Who failed who?!' – and didn't.

Between her eighteenth and twentieth year of life, Linda had three times attempted suicide; and failed. Even a deadly and well-calculated combination of atropin and barbiturates did not kill her; there were too many men in her life to come in the nick of time and save her, just as Emily had predicted.

Dear John,

Did I tell you I wrote all my A-level essays in verse? In perfect iambs, dactyls, trochees, and even anapaests – and try them in Czech, or English! You see, I wasn't morbid – just frozen. The examiners went wild, and so did I, once I entered the university, the Charles University to be precise, right in the heart of the Old Town, near the river.

I celebrated my eighteenth birthday by relinquishing my virginity to the sweetest guy imaginable, became pregnant and drove him away by having a light-hearted, easy, legal abortion, brushing the indignities and implications of it away like a summer's dust. Between suicides, I slept around for all it was worth, I just couldn't say no to anybody who gave me that look, that look which meant that I wasn't ugly any more. That although I could never be beautiful, I've grown into a desirable, or as they said, madly attractive young woman who had men trailing her scent wherever she went. But the feeling that look gave me was about the only thing I liked in lovemaking, the actual sex I found about as messy, smelly and painful as menstruations. I wouldn't want to be a young woman again for anything in the world, never!

Poor Ben Strizlik, with his Czech name and ,English upbringing; he had no idea he was marrying a frigid tramp. He didn't even know what his name meant in English, he had never bothered to look it up! I told him the first time I met him, at an international students' conference where we were both working as interpreters, and he was so delighted that he decided to marry me. Two little wrens building a nest above a socialist land full of fresh promise! The year was 1961 and a whole vista of hope was unfolding, even the tragedies less than a decade old seemed to bear fruit, not threat. My friend Olga was allowed to do a correspondence course in mathematics, and my aunts in the village, my mother's unmarried sisters as you may remember, who just a few years before hated the communists to death for taking away the little land they had, were finding cooperative farming quite a decent way to make a living. Hating the communists nevertheless, of course, but not to death, not with the lynching noose in their hearts any more.

Ben was a funny one. His ancestors were Viennese Austrians with some Czech and Jewish blood in their veins, a combination which, I suppose, may have been responsible for both their success in banking and the thin socialist streak that ran through the generations. They had moved to England at the end of the last century and never changed their name, which must have sounded to the English like two razorblades scratching each other. Ben inherited the socialist streak, broke away from his father, went to study Czech in Glasgow and, though he never learned it properly, being rather unyielding to foreign languages, found a job as an interpreter at the headquarters of the International Students' Union in Prague. Poor Ben, he never suspected how eager these people were to catch every willing soul from the West. I don't think he would admit it even now; I've heard from some people who've met him at Portsmouth Poly that he is shedding his disillusions like a dog's hair and becoming quite a neo-Stalinist.

Darling Ben, with his red hair and good manners and optimistic simplicity; he gave me a few years of near-happiness, and a daughter. Mother couldn't stand him, she said redheads were treacherous and foreigners even more so, but she did, you will remember again, love my daughter, her one and only grandchild.

Ben and I had almost everything, like most of our friends did: an almost elegant apartment, an almost new car, an almost perfect relationship. Whatever his job was, mine was almost honest; I was poetry editor on a literary magazine which was almost successful in beating censorship, and after the memorable event of the first Kafka Conference in 1963 my near-happiness was almost complete. Ben had come to respect – well, almost – my inability to share a bed and the reverse gear of my lovemaking, with its climax, if any, preceding the actual act. He didn't even look at another woman, and I was almost faithful too. Our daughter Franti- shka was bliss, and pretty, dear John, pretty as a picture.

If only something – some dark coiling worm I had kissed off Jan's face in that coffin, or possibly I'd inherited from that unhappy woman who was my father's mother – had not been eating its way through my veins towards my ice- capped heart!

I haven't told you, have I, that my father's mother had become quite a witch in her old age. As a child, I was about the only one who was not afraid of her, the people in the village crossed their hearts and spat over their shoulders at the mere sight of her. She pissed like a horse: standing upright, her legs under her long skirts slightly apart, the hot stream falling noisily to the ground, the steam and stench of it rising high. Bulls and ganders ate from her hand and butterflies dropped dead in her breath; and I am neither lying nor imagining. She died when I was six, she fell in front of the church like a tree struck by lightning and the priest told my father that she died with my name on her lips, but without the blessings of the Church.

John dearest, I wish I knew where are the ends and the beginnings of a life! And I wish – oh, how I wish it! – that I could live in this cold cottage on this lonely old mountain for the rest of my natural life, whatever that may be. But it's not mine, it's not even near-mine, and anyhow, I shall have to come down to earn some blasted money again. Now that I have you to think of and be accountable to, I don't believe I could beg any more. I did, you know. I would not accept a penny from Ben, but I would grab any other charitable hand, wear that red flannel dress with yellow and green parrots on it as if nothing was the matter with it. Don't ask me why. I suppose I was some sort of a cripple, and blamed it on England.

I don't want to leave here, I am dreading it.

Come and watch the sunrise with me, oh do come! The thrushes are already flying about making their ridiculous noises, but up on the hill there will be none. We may wake a wren up; that would be delightful. You are here with me, aren't you, John?

L.

4

John Brett, an old Canadian bum and no-gooder, his eyes the fire colour of best amber, was walking his way across the waters of the Atlantic Ocean, unable to sit quiet for five minutes in the jumbo jet seat allocated to him, driving the stewardesses and other passengers mad.

He had rolled up the sleeves of his voluminous shirt high above the elbows and the pale red hair and fiery freckles on his arms were catching the sunlight, throwing tiny dancing reflections about the polished interior of the aircraft as he paced up and down the aisles.

Thus the flight was turning rapidly into that rare event when everybody on board was sincerely grateful for the occasional powerful turbulence – which meant that John Brett was captured by the only male steward and the tallest of the stewardesses and safety-belted to his seat.

In such brief moments of rest John Brett had shut his eyes, but the lights in his face were not switched off, for he kept his broad smile on and the engagingly white teeth were flashing between the silvery yellow moustache and the still predominantly red beard.

Strangely enough, no one took the man for an idiot, not even for a childish simpleton. Some sort of a lucky fellow, a nuisance perhaps and not quite an angel as one little girl thought him to be, but pretty damn' near to what angels must have been before the Holy Church took them over. Or before they fell. Or, for that matter, just after they did.

It never occurred to them that the man could be some-body's happy dream. No more, no less.

5

'Dick dear,' said Honorah Owen, herself a PhD, to her professor husband, 'you are being bad-mannered again.'

'Fiddlesticks,' answered Richard Owen absent-mindedly and continued to stare Linda down.

'Dear Miss Wren,' sighed Honorah and shook her wiry grey curls, 'aren't we being too frightfully English for you, Dick and I?'

'Not at all,' said Linda.

'You,' pronounced Dick accusingly and screwed his index finger into Linda's shoulder, quite painfully, 'you were missing!'

Honorah sighed again. 'That is quite true, I must say.'

'You,' went on Dick, 'could have walked to Tan-y-Bwlch station, hardly more than three miles if you took the shortcut across the fields, and boarded the steam train to Blaenau. From there it's child's play to get to London.'

'But she couldn't have known that the little railway is running from April on, now could she!' his wife put in mildly.

Dick took his finger off Linda's shoulder to light a small cigar. Puffing vehemently, he watched the smoke rise towards the clear sky.

'There were a quarter of a million people on that Easter peace march, and busloads of them from Wales! Now if the Czechs keep sitting on their arses, we can shout against the Russian missiles in their back gardens as much as we want and we will only be making bloody fools of ourselves!'

He picked up a large bag, bent his head and buckled his

knees to get his tall figure into the doorway, and entered the cottage. Looking back over his shoulder, he added with a grin:

'She's good on Kafka, though.'

Not much later, but the blaze of the fire already comfortably low, Dick and Linda were sipping wine, occupying an armchair each, while Honorah busied herself in the kitchen, having resolutely rejected Linda's help.

Linda cleared her throat, overcoming a distaste for explaining herself.

'I am not a Czech, professor.'

'What?'

'I would have thought you'd understand. . . .'

'Fiddlesticks!' shouted Dick, waving his cigar. 'Nationality is a natural condition of man and has nothing to do with governments! So you don't have a Czech passport. So what?'

'That's not what I meant. I don't feel . . . I've lost touch, dammit. Right this moment, I don't feel like anything.'

'Aaah!' The professor's eyes under the white mane of hair sparkled. 'Do I detect Kafka's perfect agony? "What do I have in common with Jews, I who have nothing in common with myself?" Beautiful, but useless.'

Honorah brought in a steaming hot baking tray with a roast leg of lamb and sauté potatoes. Her face was flushed and beaming with the contentment this old place always brought out in her.

'Is the old dog barking again? Don't mind him, dear.'

Linda felt a sharp prick of envy as the professor summed up their conversation to his wife, puffing and coughing in between words; it was obviously a custom of their lifelong companionship. Honorah listened with vivid interest and dismissed the problem with a laugh.

'I am Irish-American, as you may recall, Dick. Do I feel like one? I feel English, I talk English, I cook English. It was not a decision . . . just a slow, natural drift.'

'Thank you,' said Linda.

'Dear John,' Linda scribbled, kneeling by her bed at midnight, full of wine and that delicious meal, 'this is going to be difficult. Wish you were here in flesh. Oh sorry dearest! – it's this sudden exposure to familiarities of life, wine-and-dine style. Couldn't you though, if I asked you nicely, do a bit of poltergeisting for me? Scare these two lovely people away?

L.

PS Don't bother dear. They don't scare.'

'Opening time!' Honorah's dry little voice carried surprisingly well across the meadow. Dick and Linda had filled the buckets with water some time ago, and they stood by the stream basking in the cool pink light of the declining sun.

'Literature,' croaked Dick as the weight of a bucketful of water caught him unawares, 'is no excuse for non-involvement.'

'I am involved, in my own way,' said Linda feebly, not knowing whether she was lying or not, and splashed water all over her trouser leg as she tried to keep pace with the old man's long strides.

'Your way, my way, his way, her way! It's got to be *our* way, don't you understand a simple necessity? This is a mad world, and we may either cover our faces and die, which – although it highly probably will be a mass event – is always an individual act; or we can get collectively mad at it, in an organized way, and do something!'

'Like what . . .' breathed Linda to herself, but Dick heard her all right and put the bucket down with a thud.

'Listen, young lady. . . !' He checked his anger and peered into Linda's rebelling eyes in his sharpest lecture-room manner. 'How would you define a nuclear weapon?'

Oh, buzz off, thought Linda, pursuing a noisy flock of jackdaws flying down towards the valley; oh mercy.

'Immoral,' she fired blindly.

'Why?' Dick shot back.

'I don't know. . . . Sinful may be a better word. I mean ultimate sin, beyond "Thou shall not kill", beyond greed even. Man thinking himself God? Releasing powers he

69

cannot control, thinking he can? With no other justification but self-righteousness?'

Dick picked up the bucket again and trudged towards the cottage, where, in a halo of sunshine, Honorah was waiting with three gin and tonics on a tray.

'Interesting,' he murmured on his way, 'useless but interesting.'

They took their drinks to Stalin's shoe and surveyed the golden valley, the glittering mist above the ocean and the mountains now beheaded by black and scarlet sunset clouds, Linda silent and wistful, Dick repeating their talk for his wife's benefit.

'You know that this blessed mountain is one of the few places the bomb is unlikely to destroy?' Honorah said contentedly.

Linda shivered.

'It's getting chilly, isn't it?' continued the eager-faced woman happily. 'Evenings are always chilly here, even in the peak of summer. No stuffiness, no sweat; cool and peaceful.'

'I have a daughter in Paris,' Linda said and wished, for a long enough moment, that she'd travelled to that confounded peace march in London.

'Paris!' exclaimed Honorah and rubbed her cheek against her husband's shoulder, 'Do you remember, darling, do you. . . ?'

'That's where we met, at la Sorbonne,' explained the professor drily but with a twinkle in his eye. 'I wandered in on her lecture about eighteenth-century Utopianism and thought she was useless, but really rather pretty.'

'It was my first lecture, dear,' sighed Honorah and her whole face swam like a water-lily on a pond of bliss.

'Dear John,' wrote Linda by candlelight, 'will you marry me?' She frowned furiously, tore the page in two and cried herself to sleep.

Dick made the breakfast. The toast was burnt, but the eggs and bacon were their English best.

70

'Are you a socialist?' he asked, eyeing Linda with sudden suspicion.

'I suppose I am,' answered Linda and wished he hadn't asked. Dick, however, merely gave out a delighted chuckle.

'Welcome to the family,' said Honorah, and they both chuckled like schoolchildren until, quite against her will, Linda laughed too.

'If you call me "professor" once again, I'll wring your neck. Is "Dick" too much to ask? One single syllable?'

'And it's "Honey" for me, nothing to do with the sweet sticky stuff, just a silly family tradition. But then, Honorah is quite a mouthful, too much to ask from anybody.'

'Linda,' said Linda.

The three of them were giving the old Land Rover a wax polish with gusto, as if they hadn't spent a tiresome day filling the worst holes in the track with broken slate from the small quarry up in the forest.

'I wonder if John will make it up here,' said Dick, and Linda's heart missed a beat, drummed up, and missed another.

'He may,' Honey straightened her back with a groan, 'and he may not. I am sure Linda would take good care of him should he arrive after we left. But I think we ought to drive to town tomorrow, load this old thing with provisions and pack the freezer tight, just in case, Dick dear.'

'Righty-ho,' agreed Dick. 'John is a man who enjoys his food – if he can get it.'

'Who-is-he?' breathed Linda.

'John? Oh, he is an absolute dream, he won't bother you.'

'Useless,' said Dick fondly, 'except with his hands; watch him work with wood or stone and the world clicks in place.'

Linda almost howled. 'But who is he?'

'John Brett?' Honorah's eyes went all soft and misty. 'He is a man we met on a hike through Nova Scotia. We got lost a bit and it started to rain and we were quite desperate – he gave us shelter in his cabin.'

Dick laughed. 'Only it wasn't his at all, and the rightful

71

owners were about to kick up a hell of a fuss when they found him, and us, there. . . .'

'But darling, that was before they had a look around. . . .'

'I said they were about to! They didn't, of course. While squatting there, John had rebuilt the fireplace, carved the backs of all the chairs and the legs of the table in a most beautiful pattern, cleaned up the well and roofed it over, and chopped enough dead wood to last for three hard winters in a row.'

'They let us off very lightly indeed, and John spent the rest of the hike with us, and we told him about the *hafodty* and how we can stay here only for Easter and in August for about three weeks each year because of our commitments and how the place is therefore falling to pieces. . . .'

'And he looked so sad, remember? He kept shaking his head, like a man wounded. That's when he promised to come one Easter and "do the remedies". Isn't that what he called it? Remedies?'

'Yes, dear. Only he never has come so far. Being of no fixed abode, as he said, we couldn't write to him. But he sent a postcard now and then, the last one about a month ago. . . .'

'Six weeks, Honey, six weeks.'

'So you see, Linda dear, he is a dream, but not entirely. I wish we could stay longer, just to give it a chance. But we have to go the day after tomorrow, there is a London Peace Conference we mustn't miss.'

Linda grabbed at that, like a falling mountaineer at a rope. 'Maybe I should go too, to the conference, I mean? What with all the conversations we had . . . I'd like to take part. . . .'

'Fiddlesticks,' said Dick, 'you wish no such thing. A white lie, my dear girl, but useless. You just stay right where you are, and scribble on. It seems to suit you, and it's fine with us.'

Just stay where you are? I've heard this one before, and look what it did to me, Linda wanted to scream – but didn't.

She spent the next two days in a state of suspended

animation. The weather had changed, it was raining cats and dogs; Richard Owen sat most of the time – apart from the promised catering trip to the town of Porthmadog – by the fire, cursed under his breath and worked on a draft of his new paper, 'Kafka – an Exile' – inspired, he said, by Linda's foolish remarks. Honorah Owen retired to the little upstairs study and, humming to herself, corrected the proofs of the book on Utopianism with which she hoped to crown her academic career before retiring.

Linda Strizlik/Wren crouched in her bed and brushed her lower lip with her little finger.

The two dear Owens finally departed in the shuddering, groaning Land Rover. Linda pulled herself together.

'Dear John,' she wrote, 'nothing, nothing will make me stop loving you, least of all somebody else's dream.

L.'

'I wonder,' said Honey after the old Land Rover was successfully steered into its garage in Ealing and they'd both relaxed and lit a small cigar each, 'I really do wonder what made you stare at Linda so badly when we arrived at the *hafodty*, Dick dear. Surely you were not mad that she didn't come to London for the peace march!'

'I don't know. I think I was, for a while. But you are right, there was something else.'

'I wonder. . . .'

'She's changed, that's it. She's changed. Looks much, much better, sort of, yet somewhat peculiar. Can't say why.'

'It's the eyes, Dick. Oh I've seen those changeable blue-black-green eyes before, lots of people have them in Europe, but not with bright amber specks.'

'Bright amber? Like John's?'

'Yes, Dick dear. Like John's.'

That night Linda dreamt about her mother being very angry at her in the kitchens of a huge castle-hotel, because she,

Linda, was unable to cook a decent soup for the queens and kings assembled above. Linda wanted to make it up with mother by playing a violin, really rather well, but mother snatched the instrument from her, broke it over the edge of a stove, unhooked a small iron door and fed the broken wood to the flames.

Immediately after that, the kitchens and some adjoining gothic arcades filled with people; there were some old relatives and unknown young children among them, but most of the crowd were Linda's generation, men and women she had met in life, far too many of them. Linda went from group to group, getting involved in meals, quarrels, wife swopping, gossip, political plots, childbirths, heart attacks, endless secretive gestures; getting crowded, exhausted, losing all hope.

She woke up with the desperate knowledge that only by supreme effort would she be able to maintain some relationship with John the fisherman, the violin maker, the postcard painter, the dream.

Days passed, even weeks, and nothing happened – apart from all that flutter and song in the air, mating, tiny pregnancies, nesting, hatching of eggs, and replacement of the daffodils by the foxgloves. The morning after the Owens left, glorious weather came, and it stayed glorious for weeks; Linda grew wearily addicted to sunbathing and to talking to herself.

One day a solitary man with a rucksack on his back appeared in the distance and quickly re-entered the forest. Linda's heart did funny tricks for the rest of that day. She could not bring herself to trek down to the village: guiltily, she fed from the freezer.

Most of the time she composed letters to John in her head, and often spoke them out loud, but she felt unable actually to write them down as she used to. She had tried once, but stopped writing right after the 'Dearest John' bit, filled with profound embarrassment. It felt as if John had got married to somebody else, and further correspondence was uncalled for.

At night, while burning dry prickly gorse twigs in the

fireplace, more for light and sound than for warmth, Linda began to perceive her solitude as loneliness. An acute loneliness, a desire for somebody to arrive, even if it were a dream shatterer, a ruddy man with scornful eyes.

One such night, when the last twigs, consumed by flickering flames, had instantly disintegrated into a heap of black ashes, Linda was struck by an awful truth: all her people were dead! None of the old people, people she belonged to, were left, there were not even some forgotten cousins; Václav was an only child, and all Emily's sisters had remained unmarried and died childless. Brother Jan was sharing the grave with mother and father, and sister Hela was either dead, or undead. . . .

Linda ran outside and stood under the stars, all the absurd thousands of them cluttered together in one sky yet held apart by visible forces. Timidly she called out her sister's name. There wasn't any response, apart from a muffled flapping of a startled woodpigeon's wings; yet by and by, something did seep through the twinkle and flit of the stars: an urgency. An unfinished quarrel. An interrupted communion. A whiff of Hela's cigarette, the signal of her despair. A hint of a perfume, the sign of her happiness. A glimpse of a distance, yet, at the same time, a look over a shoulder, a look so close Linda could almost touch it.

She slept well that night. She lay on her back, stretched out and motionless, the way Hela always used to sleep. And if she had dreams, she remembered nothing of them in the morning – only a vague feeling of things white, clear and pleasantly cold like sheets of ice over an entire landscape.

No more idleness. Linda sat down to write the uncomfortable story of her sister Hela. She owed it to her, like she owed something to one and each of her old people, like she owed it to herself. Compared with such urgency, the lack of an address seemed a matter of trifling importance.

Linda had finished the story just before Angharad drove in her cattle – twenty head of them, cows, heifers and bullocks, all ebony-black but one – to graze on the fields, and life began to speed up, spin and whirl.

Sister Hela

The very first memory Linda could recollect of her big sister Hela was glimpses of her knees. Linda was fidgeting on a stool placed on the pavement outside the house, she had a saucepan on her head covering most of her face and hopefully her ears, and her sister was cutting her hair. It was a sunny day, because her head felt hot and if she lowered her eyes she could see the sunshine dancing on her lap and in the long blonde curls that fell and fell to the ground. Now and then she could see her sister's knees, they were square and knobbly and there was a dark blue scar on one of them.

Hela seemed to have a thing about hair. She loved to tousle and pull her brother Jan's, and she never missed an opportunity to brush and comb and brush again her mother's fine dark hair, thin but long. Hela loved Emily! She loved her mother with a totally unselfish but enormous, passionate love. She considered herself fortunate, because Emily suffered all her approaches with good humour and visible affection, and never pushed her away as she would little Linda; she knew that her mother trusted her and approved of her, though she truly loved only one person in the world, her beautiful and doomed son Jan.

At the end of the war, when Hela was just turning sweet sixteen, she was given her first flower-print frock with short sleeves and a pleated skirt, with matching pink socks and shoes with heels. Rose-cheeked and breathless, her arms full of lilac blossoms, she climbed onto the tank that backed into Quick Street. And that's how she got her first – and really rather powerful – kiss from a man, an elderly Russian sergeant with one empty sleeve and one crushingly strong arm. Tears spurted from her eyes and her lip had split, but then everybody was crying and screaming and getting their skins cut on the armour and their noses bleeding in scuffles over climbing on to the tank to shake hands with the liberators.

A kiss is only a kiss, but this one may well have been ominous. Even little Linda noticed how bright-eyed Hela was, how she pranced about, and how long it took for the lip to heal.

Hela seemed to go right on dancing, all through the summer, and the winter, and the next spring. Then the pretty frock vanished from the wardrobe and was replaced by a pair of coarse trousers, a straight skirt and a couple of uniform shirts with emblems of communist youth stitched to their sleeves. She took her art school far more seriously; went from meeting to meeting, took on evening classes in dialectical materialism, and dismissed her current boyfriend, whom Emily rather liked, for being lukewarm to the great cause of communism.

Emily was getting worried. The girl was coming home late, smelling of cigarettes, and snapping at her father. With the exception of her mother, the girl seemed to abhor anybody and anything that wasn't Young. Freedom was Young, the Republic was Young, the Revolution was Young. She was secretly furious that her father had been given a party card: wasn't the party supposed to be Young, too? It was all right to be old if one was a Leader, but that of course was absolutely out of her father's reach; poor Václav did not know what Marxism was! He could not even pronounce the word 'Dialectic' properly! In the end, Emily had to give Hela a proper talking to. Her father might be uneducated and not very intelligent and with no initiative whatsoever, but he worked hard and as best he could and the party might well do with more like him. Emily would not have her sneer at her father! Hela nodded and did her best to be polite; but she was seldom at home.

Two years later, things had changed. The party had won, even though it wasn't exactly Young and there wasn't much of a proper Revolution. Hela had broken up with another boyfriend because he went on saying that the whole thing was nothing but a coup organized by the Soviets, and that from now on true Revolution, their own Revolution, was dead. But she cried a lot; she missed him.

One of Emily's unmarried sisters, aunt Anna, came from the village to stay for a month and do some sewing for the family; she was an accomplished needlewoman. She made a lovely dress for Hela and, to her mother's great satisfaction, the girl was thrilled and kissed her aunt on both cheeks. Despite the fact that Anna, a stubborn peasant, could not even say 'communist' without spitting on the floor!

Emily didn't want Hela to go to one of those voluntary youth labour camps she was so keen on. Why not go to the village with Anna and help with the harvest? Surely the republic needed the corn more than yet another dam; and she would be well looked after and there wouldn't be any doubtful characters around. But Hela laughed and danced off, or rather bounced off, on the back of a lorry. When she returned home three months later she was emaciated, her hair was thin and her skin had an unhealthy, dirty look. For weeks and weeks on end she was silent and anxiously hygienic.

Emily had bad suspicions, but because sex and related matters were still taboo in her book she didn't dare to ask. She had been very tired herself, and finally she agreed to go to a sanatorium to have her TB treated. After she returned, all seemed well with her elder daughter.

Hela was pretty again, though her pleasing plumpness was gone. She had graduated from her art school with the highest honours and immediately got a job on a new magazine, *Socialist Woman*, as an art editor. At the age of twenty she had become exactly the kind of young woman Emily had always wanted her to be: well-read, well-spoken, nicely mannered, and all set for an unpretentious but steady success. The kind of woman Emily would have wanted to be herself, and could have been, had she been born richer, or much later.

Everyone liked Hela. She was nice to be with, and a model comrade. She was reliable, never stepped out of the party line, yet had a certain artistic flavour. Hela Střízlík was a decent girl, her friends would say, and they would keep close to her, because she had a ruthless ability to make everything around her look decent. Dark Stalinist horrors were raging in and around the party: people were bewildered, humiliated, jailed by the thousand and hanged by the dozen. Yet Hela would merely set her teeth and go on decorating and preening the small world of her office and home, working hard on improving the visual image of *Socialist Woman*, and sit through the party meetings with lowered eyes and hands clasped firmly in her lap. Emily quite agreed. If everybody would make up their minds to be decent, the whole people's democracy would soon turn out decent too.

If only Hela could keep a man! At the age of twenty-five she had been married and divorced three times! Few people in the neighbourhood ever noticed; Hela did not believe in big weddings, the marriages were registered in different districts of Prague, and as there weren't any children the divorces were a mere formality. Or so Hela said. But each time she came back home again she smoked like hell, her hands shook and she snapped at everyone, sometimes even at her mother. Emily was appalled; she just did not know how to help her daughter. But at least Hela seemed happy in her career; nothing would make her turn sloppy in her work, or about her person, or make her blame something or somebody else for her own unhappiness. Anyway, things were much worse with Jan, and if Emily had a dozen hearts, and a dozen lives, she would have given them all to him.

Then Jan shot himself. And something irreplaceable went missing in each of them. Václav and Emily, Hela and Linda, they each suffered separately, and without much pity for each other.

It took Emily two more years to understand what was the trouble with Hela: she desperately wanted children but despite years of treatment and all the best doctors' efforts she could not conceive; but she would not tell anyone in case there was still a chance. And for the shame of it. From then on, Emily pitied her daughter enormously, and hated the whole breed of men, of which Jan had been such a rare exception.

There had never been much true sisterly love lost between Linda and Hela; they were too far apart, and too different. When Linda was little Hela liked to buy her presents and dress her up; she would even have coats made for her by her tailor. But then Linda had grown into a troublesome, pimply, touchy teenager, and sneered at her elegant, confident sister. And when she hatched out of her ugly duckling's shell she went quite wild for a while, and so unlike Hela, or Emily, that it was sometimes difficult even to talk to her.

At the tender age of eighteen Linda went to a hospital to have her light-hearted abortion. Emily tried to keep Hela from knowing, but the secret got out and Hela stormed into the hospital just after Linda had had her bath and shave. For an hour, she pleaded with her; she cried; she fell on her knees and begged Linda to carry the child. Hela would then adopt it, love it, adore it, give it everything under the sun, never let anyone hurt it. 'I love the baby,' she cried, 'I love it now, I won't let you destroy it!'

Linda was very pale, but all she had to say was that there were enough abandoned gypsy babies for Hela to choose from, if she really wanted to adopt a child. Hela screamed, but a nurse came and took Linda away; her turn in the abortion queue had come.

Hela never wanted to see her sister again.

The 1960s came, and decency seemed to have won, or was at least winning. *Socialist Woman* was beginning to look vaguely like a women's magazine, and the concept of private property had been rehabilitated. Hela was buying her own brand-new apartment, and a car, and a cottage in a tiny hamlet by one of the prettiest little rivers of southern Bohemia. Ticklish currents of liberalization were beginning to ruffle the party rank and file, but Hela merely set her teeth and continued to expand and beautify her private kingdom, her decency niche, and sit through party meetings with lowered eyes and a silent little smile on her lips.

Baby Frantishka came into the world and Emily would often bring her to Hela's apartment or to her cottage in the country. For a few hours or days the two women would pretend that Frantishka was Hela's baby, not Linda's. The pretty little girl was soon calling Hela her mummy and her own mother mum. She brought the sisters together again, if not very close.

At last, Hela was having her share in true life's happiness. She had found her dream man, a sweet-natured and handsome fashion photographer with artistic ambitions, younger than herself and gentle as a child.

He adored her, and let her love him to her heart's desire. They went to the Adriatic Sea each summer, and each time Hela returned looking younger and unbearably glamorous with her slim figure, deep suntan and eyes lit by happiness.

For six long years her colleagues, the women in charge of *Socialist Woman*, had to endure her old-fashioned and belated bliss. Each time they were invited to Hela's apartment for one of her regular dinner parties they would survey the beautiful furniture, the works of art, the collection of antiques, the elegant food, and the manifest devotion of her young husband; and there would be a vindictive envy in their comradely hearts. But she was oblivious to evil.

The year of Dubček was a year of reckoning. Amidst the dust of the battle between the conservatives and the progressives in the party, many an old score was paid off, and woe to the comrades who failed to put up their defences. Hela was certainly not paying attention, and the attack took her completely by surprise.

During a party meeting in March she was accused of being a conservative, a hardliner; of having been a Stalinist; of having always led an immoral life; of having initiated the political persecution of a talented young poet by framing him as a source of her VD twenty years ago; of having misused her proletarian origins to gain personal and material advantage.

Hela sat through the accusations looking at her hands, clasped so firmly in her lap that their knuckles were white. She did not defend herself, and the attention soon switched to other culprits. Nothing much came out of it, there were much bigger fish to fry and everybody at that meeting could have been accused of similar things and some of much worse; but although Hela was merely demoted to being an assistant art editor, and remained a party member, her life lay in ruins.

Rumours of the meeting travelled quickly. Nobody came to Hela's dinner parties; she had become an embarrassment. Her young husband grew fidgety, and started to sulk. Hela had clung to him too much, he said; he felt manipulated. Besides, they were too different politically. And he wanted children. Hela cried out in pain and he quickly collected a few belongings and left the apartment, tears streaming down his face. Within a month he obtained a divorce, and a fortnight later he married a young radical student who was four months pregnant by him; and secretly regretted leaving Hela ever since.

The Prague Spring was full of divorces, like all revolutionary times. But that was no consolation to Hela. She turned to drink – but she had to drink alone. For the first time in her life she had no friends, and she couldn't possibly have known how short a period it would turn out to be.

Emily could offer very little help. She had her hands full nursing Václav, who had turned rapidly and devastatingly senile after his retirement a short while ago. He just could not come to terms with the discovery that, after more than fifty years of hard labour and twenty-odd years of party membership, his old age pension had been set at a mere quarter of a youngster's wages. He felt debased; betrayed; conspired against. He soon became incontinent.

Only once had Hela telephoned her sister, quite late at night. Linda grabbed a cab and came over, but it would have been better if she hadn't. The two of them got drunk together, and it ended in a row. Hela should leave the women's magazine, said Linda, she ought to have left a long time ago. What was a decent woman like her doing in the stupidest, crappiest, most fraudulent of all periodicals ever printed in the country?! And as for that husband of hers, it was good riddance. He had always been a gigolo; his photographs were sheer trumpery; he had no brains; he was a young idiot. If anyone was a young idiot, sobbed Hela furiously, then it was Linda. She had always been a conceited, irresponsible brat, and hadn't changed one bit. She had had all the luck. She had never had to get her hands dirty. She knew nothing about work, real responsible work, not poetry. And, above all, Linda knew nothing about love!

For a while, Hela stared at her sister with cold eyes, then pushed her to the door. 'He loved me,' she said quietly, 'he always will. Go home, you will never understand.'

Linda rang her sister next morning, apologized, and forgot all about it. She was having the time of her life. There was a whole brand-new era of democratic socialism to be taken care of, precisely by poets! And there was a little daughter to be woken up with a kiss each morning, and sung to at bedtimes. Otherwise Ben was mostly in charge of the child, and the housekeeping; he was glad to oblige. These were bewildering times for him; the usually placid Czechs seemed all to have gone mad. He was most sympathetic, but preferred to follow the developments via newspapers, magazines and television, rather than by mingling with the crowds. Linda's family had never really accepted him, they had this thing about foreigners. He never bothered to ingratiate himself; but now Frantishka kept asking to see her 'mummy', so he invited Hela to lunch.

She excused herself once or twice, but finally she came. The place was quite a mess and she spent half the time cleaning up. Frantishka got bored and ran off to play in the yard. What a tragic woman, Ben thought, watching Hela move about the flat and smoke endlessly; and for a brief moment he wished he was back in England, where passions did not run all that deep, and private life was kept well apart from politics.

When a year later Emily died of a heart attack, it was Hela who did the decent thing. She locked up her beautiful apartment and moved into Little Quick Street to nurse, feed and wash her poor old father who was terrified of her, thinking she was the grand duchess he used to fear so much as a child. The five days spent dealing with Václav's thin weak shit were like purgatory to Hela, and she needed it.

But creaking and grating, lamenting and rasping, the wheel of history had turned back nevertheless. Dubček was out, the Russians firmly in. Hela was fully rehabilitated, given back her superior position as chief art editor with profound apologies from her colleagues, and was greatly sought after by her friends. She accepted all this with good grace, for she could not imagine her life without the magazine; it was, after all, her baby, she had been with it from the very start. But she could not help feeling dirty.

She grieved when Ben took little Frantishka away to England. She knew that Linda would soon have to follow her daughter, while the going was still good. Yet Frantishka might be much better off and Linda . . . Linda was no use to Hela. Never would be. Perhaps it was nobody's fault. Perhaps they weren't real sisters after all. Emily had joked about it often enough; perhaps she was being serious.

Emily! With Emily gone, all love was gone.

During Emily's funeral, the sisters stood shoulder to shoulder; the entire neighbourhood was there, weeping, whispering, watching. Václav sat in a wheelchair kindly provided by the old warden of the Tree Park cemetery, a retired gardener himself who was always fond of Václav, although – being an obdurate Catholic – he had had awesome quarrels with him. Václav seemed asleep, his head, with its wrinkled yellow skin and sporadic tufts of white hair, looking like a dead chicken's. Nobody knew when he passed away, but he was certainly dead by the time the first handfuls of earth were thrown into the grave, drumming and rattling on the wooden coffin lid. Like a faithful dog, the neighbours nodded fondly, like the faithful dog he was.

He was taken straight to the mortuary and the sisters sat with him waiting for the doctor to arrive, silently searching their separate hearts as to why on earth they had loathed and scorned their meek and harmless father so much.

They thought of Jan and were glad they had had him cremated; the urn with his ashes was now in his dead mother's arms. It took a little conspiracy and a lot of bribery to arrange it, but Linda was good at conspiracy and Hela was never short of money.

Now and then, they smiled at each other. Linda often

tortured herself throughout the years that followed: if only, in that pleasant morgue smelling of lime blossom and chalk, she and Hela had tried harder! Maybe they were afraid that, if they uttered even one word, the floodgates would open and they would howl and wail with grief. Emily would have disapproved strongly of such behaviour. Emily was dead, and more than ever commanded simple dignity. She would have liked her funeral, though: it was neither overdone nor underdone, everybody's grief was genuine and friendly, the old cemetery looked spick and span and hundreds of wee candles flickered and flittered away, as if it was All Souls' Eve.

The doctor came and Hela made it clear that she was in charge. Linda got up and made for the door, touching her sister's shoulder as she went. I love you, she whispered. Hela looked up and her lips moved soundlessly: me too. But then the doctor asked a question, Hela turned back to answer it, and the moment was lost forever.

All Linda had to remember it by were six picture post-cards from Prague with Hela's elegant scrawl on them, one for each Christmas. But Frantishka had a whole bookcase full of photographic albums and picture books about Prague that her aunt kept sending her until she stopped and nobody knew why. For a long time they didn't; and even afterwards they were only guessing.

On 9 May 1975 a glittering throng of diplomats and generals, newly decorated heroes of socialist labour, masters of sports, artists of national merit, actors, opera singers, pop stars, academics, party functionaries and selected representatives of women and youth, was mounting the gala staircase of Prague Castle to celebrate, at a lavish banquet provided by the government, the thirtieth anniversary of the Liberation of Czechoslovakia by the Glorious Red Army.

There was some pushing and shoving in the line-up for the handshake with the President and his wife, and some jostling around the enticing buffet tables, but on the whole it was a dignified event. Security was unobtrusive and drinks were plentiful. Hela Střízlík, who was just turning forty-six but seemed ageless in her glamorous evening gown, looked on wistfully. She could not afford to drink, not in public anyway, especially not in this kind of public. She was a bit of an alcoholic, but a very private, decent one. An East German diplomat to whom she was talking in his native language, and who was oblivious to her problem, had got hold of a whole bottle of delicious sparkling wine from the Crimea, the famous Soviet champagne, and kept pestering her with it, thrusting a glass into her hand, proposing toasts. Finally, just to get rid of him, she drank.

'Hela?'

She spun round and there he was, her sweet husband, her lover of another time, another place, another world. He had no business being there – he was supposed to have become an outcast, a dissident, on account of his radical young wife who had already spent two years in prison.

He looked shabby enough, unshaven and ruffled and wearing an incongruous combination of dinner jacket and jeans. With trained eyes, Hela picked up the nearest security man; he did not seem to be bothered so far. Go away, she pleaded, but it was the East German diplomat who took off, too drunk to be offended.

There was but one thing to do, before they got wise to him. Hela gathered her skirts and walked gracefully through the magnificent castle rooms towards the hall and down the gala staircase, across the marble-paved courtyard and out under the arch, hoping he would follow, hoping he was real.

She had not been seen again.

It is practically impossible to vanish in such a small country with no coast, where everyone is constantly re-registered and accounted for and no one can go abroad without special permission obtainable only after months of bureaucratic procedure and security screening. Therefore it was concluded that Hela must have been involved in that dreadful accident in the Prague underground railway which happened later that month. The cause of the explosion remained unknown, or undisclosed, but the results were whispered everywhere. Several carriages of the midnight train had been burning in a tunnel for hours, and such bodies as were found were charred beyond positive identification.

Before this conclusion was reached, however, Linda got a letter from the Czechoslovak Embassy in London politely inquiring whether or not the whereabouts of her sister, Comrade Hela Střízlík, were known to her. And that's how she was eventually told that Hela had disappeared.

Time is a strange thing, she thought, once you start measuring it. Hela was twelve when Linda was born; and Frantishka was twelve when Hela died. But maybe she had not died, maybe in another twelve years she might come back from wherever she was. She never cheated.

6

John Brett was getting tired of England and Wales. In fact he was getting tired of himself. He was growing middle-aged, he was no longer curious to see new landscapes or eager to meet new people or gluttonous for new sensual and extra-sensual experiences. So what, by the soul of Kerouac, was he still doing on the road?

A small pick-up truck passed, and stopped. Brett caught up with it and the driver motioned him to climb into the back, even though he was alone in the cabin. That's right, buddy, thought Brett as the vehicle jerked forward and he bounced against the side, why gab? Why swop lies?

He shouldn't have gone to the Owens in London. They fussed and fretted, and didn't know at all what to do with him. It was one thing to hike with a six-foot taciturn Canadian through a few square miles of Nova Scotia, quite another to entertain him in an English family home full of books, musical instruments and antique china. Brett chuckled. Obviously they thought that he was one of the last wild men roaming the forests of the north who have never seen even the façade of a university, let alone a map of Europe or an embroidered napkin!

The truck had climbed a hill; left and right of the narrow gravel road, from horizon to horizon, lay the moor, quiet and empty, like fossilized tidal waves covered in fuzzy mould. Brett shut his eyes. He had been to places like this a hundred thousand times. He had had a hundred thousand years of it. The heat and the chill were in his bones. He curled up against his rucksack and slept.

The trouble with cattle, thought Angharad, is that they won't be rushed. It takes them a whole day to march a few miles! Angharad was a competent farmer, but she was still impatient and frustrated by sluggishness, even by simple slowness: the ages grass takes to grow, for example, or the time snow takes to melt. But there was pleasure in the simplicity, the peremptory nature of the task; she usually had to work from dawn to dusk in all directions. And it was nice to walk behind her own herd; watching the changing pattern the white cow was creating by moving backwards and forwards among the ebony-black rest of them; talking to the dogs. The four young ones were running to and fro, up and down, overdoing everything; but she let them – working sheepdogs rarely had much fun. It made the old bitch anxious, though, and she kept glancing at Angharad with disapproving eyes. Come on, old girl, laughed Angharad, this isn't sheepwork, it's more like a procession, pilgrimage of the beast; be kind to the puppies.

Above Tan-y-Bwlch Angharad turned her herd sharply to the right, onto a narrow westward lane. From then on, they marched practically blind, the sun glaring straight into their eyes.

Linda was seeing ghosts. In the morning, when she was making tea in the kitchen, a great big shadow of a man swept across the whitewashed walls. She peered through the window; ran out; but there was not a soul in sight. At noon, having sweated in vain over a letter to Frantishka, she finally lay back in her deckchair and dozed off. A heavy hand squeezed her shoulder. She leaped from the chair, knocking it over. Apart from a few lazy butterflies, there was no movement anywhere.

Linda decided to treat the situation the way her mother would have done. Come what may, Emily used to say, make sure you are clean inside out. Things are much easier, if there is nothing a woman can be ashamed of, like dirty dishes in the sink, unswept floors, dusty shelves or smelly knickers. Armed with broom, brush, water, and soap, and singing those endless French folksongs she had learnt at school and still remembered word by word, Linda worked her way through the afternoon, only occasionally looking over her shoulder when she thought she heard steps, or voices.

The dream Brett was having was only a shallow one – unknown faces coming and going in a slow and endless succession – but he was sorry to lose it. The truck was now rattling through a severe little town pressed against steep slate rocks that looked as if they were scraped down with blunt knives. The brakes squealed, and the vehicle halted with a jolt. The trouble with roads, thought Brett as he threw his rucksack over the side and jumped down after it, is that they always lead somewhere, and the traveller becomes a tourist. It was not an original thought, and Brett winced: he had been having this trouble for the last couple of years, he seemed to be living out somebody else's old diary. The driver took his truck off without taking or giving a word, and dark-haired schoolchildren in neat uniforms hushed each other, staring at the giant stranger with the bushy hair and the thick red beard. An Alien from the Planet of the Fox perhaps; or somebody from the movies.

Not that Blaenau Ffestiniog was an unfriendly town: Brett was made most welcome in the pub, especially after he asked for a beer in mellow Canadian accent, and drained his pint at one expert gulp. Rounds were ordered and stories were told and soon, inevitably, he was challenged to arm wrestling. Although not tall, the Welsh were sturdy, but Brett, smiling sheepishly, defeated them all. He missed the three o'clock train; the red-on-black steam engine was puffing and pulling the pretty carriages along just as he stepped into the sunshine. But his new friends would not let him walk: a ride was organized for him in a little three-wheeler meant for invalids but driven by a young chap used to racing motorbikes.

Consequently, Brett caught up with Angharad and her cattle just in time to help her open the unyielding gate at the top of the forestry track.

The dogs took one sniff at him and became respectful. Angharad was instantly at ease; she knew a farmer when she saw one. And the cattle lowed as if they were greeting a long-lost master.

Linda heard the lowing and mooing but thought she was hallucinating again. She had washed her hair; it dried within minutes in the hot sunshine and the steadily rising, easterly wind; she was now trying to do something with it but it was flying away and crackling with static electricity. In the end she succeeded in pinning it up in an untidy knot, carefully avoiding a full look into the mirror.

She walked through the cottage and enjoyed its cleanliness and orderliness. Even her letters to John and the pages of Poor Emily, Little Linda, Joseph Stalin, Brother Jan and Sister Hela lay in neat piles on the desk in the downstairs study bedroom she had taken for her own. She had an absurd desire to tie them up in pink and blue ribbons, but of course there weren't any. It is as if I am preparing to die, she felt, and she found the thought peaceful and so well within the order of things that it was pleasing.

She put the kettle on and next instant the kitchen was full of black-and-white dogs leaping about and flashing their eyes and teeth at her, mad, laughing dogs, but obviously young and harmless. Hooves were thudding outside, a huge black head appeared in the window, a voice called, and another, and the dogs ran out again.

It's him all right, thought Linda, this is the man who threw in his shadow this morning. And squeezed my shoulder at noon.

'Any friends of Dick's and Honey's are welcome here,' said Angharad and shook Linda's hand, eyeing her with curiosity. 'Have you been here long?'

'Oh, I don't know . . . three months,' said Linda.

'Good,' nodded Angharad. 'It's a shame if the place

stands empty. It's big enough for a family.' She laughed nervously. 'I mean it's big enough for two people to live here without bumping into each other constantly.'

Brett was cursing the Owens under his breath. Why the devil hadn't they told him about the woman? Then she offered him her hand, and he had to shake it.

'Hi,' he drawled, stalling. 'I suppose I've come to keep an old promise. Sorry for butting in on you like this. I am John Brett.'

'I know,' said she, peacefully.

So she knew, did she? Brett cursed some more. What kind of a set-up was this? 'I didn't get your name.' As if it mattered.

'Oh. Sorry. I am Linda.'

'Angharad,' said Angharad.

They were as thick as thieves, John Brett and Angharad. They drank their tea in a hurry, and went into the fields. Linda took her cup to Stalin's shoe and watched them from a distance.

The wind was still rising, dry and hot, and Angharad had to hold one hand to her brow to prevent the black curly tresses of her hair from flapping across her face and eyes.

Angharad. Pharaoh's daughter running away with a great big barbarian. Linda was surprised and embarrassed. How jealous she was!

Yet she could very well guess what the two were talking about while walking up and down the fields, picking up handfuls of grass, bending over the weakening stream, looking up at the cloudless sky: the weather. It had not worried Linda unduly, but even she had noticed that all was not well: the bog had dried up and there were only a few shallow pools left in the stream where she could bathe.

As always at this time of day, an hour before sunset, the wind had suddenly dropped and, but for the maddening birdsong, the mountain and the valley were calm. Yet the clarity of the air had gone, it was thick with dust and heat. The green of the grasses was dull and streaked with yellow, and there were far too many patches of scarlet-pink all over the slopes. The foxgloves had flowered early and in unusually large numbers, tall, beautiful and poisonous. The sky was all wrong too: not only was it cloudless, it had a peculiar whitish colour like skimmed milk or dead human skin, most inappropriate for the month of May.

The black cattle seemed menacing to Linda and the solitary white cow only made it worse. They kept well together and grazed nervously, as if they too felt a menace lurking somewhere near.

For Linda this had been an altogether bewitched and bewitching day and she decided to turn in early. But first there were a few more wretched hours of twilight to be spent in various little agonies, regrets and premonitions.

'See you soon, then,' Angharad smiled at Brett, who walked her up the track to the road where her mother was already waiting in a car to drive her and the dogs back to the farm.

'What an awfully big fellow,' said Angharad's mother. 'Who is he?'

'Who are you?' asked Brett after Linda had explained to him all about the food in the freezer and where he would find the various tools he wanted. 'I mean, what do you do?'

'Nothing much.' Linda did not mean to sound off-putting, she simply couldn't think of any other answer that would not give her away, or appear preposterous. How could she say – oh, I am just walking up and down my life, picking up handfuls here and there, wondering why it's drying up. Hoping for rain.

'That makes two of us,' said Brett, giving her a friendly grin and making it clear that, as far as he was concerned, they needn't talk any further.

Linda retreated to her bedroom and bolted the door.

The moment darkness fell, the wind rose again and droned and swished till dawn, making the night a misery for such as could not sleep.

And then the thrushes woke up and the cattle walked over the fallen fence and gathered on the lawn and shat so loudly that whatever little sleep Linda had been hoping for flew into the blue.

Before long, John Brett was sitting on the roof hammering away. Linda decided that the time had come for her to go back to London and face the music – whatever that meant.

But she lingered on.

It was another uncommonly hot day. By the time John Brett came down from the roof he was soaked in sweat. The wind blew him dry within minutes; he stank like a horse. Or rather, thought Linda and blushed, like a horse who had been rolling in hay.

'Hi Linda,' he said, 'nice to have you around.'

'And you,' said Linda, truthfully.

'Everybody calls me Brett.'

Linda merely nodded but her face lit up so obviously, so handsomely, that he wondered why the deuce he had thought yesterday that she was a bloodless, prim little spinster. He had no idea what a great burden he had taken away from Linda; she couldn't have called him John, not ever, not if her soul's salvation depended on it!

From then on, for the rest of the day, she found herself following him like a lamb.

Like the newborn lamb she had not resisted the impulse to cuddle many weeks ago. She had picked it up and held it in her arms and brushed her cheeks against its cold curly wool. When she put it down again she couldn't get rid of it; it followed her on its puny, unsteady legs, bleating heart-rendingly until an angry ewe came running down the slope and claimed it.

But who was there to claim Linda back?

Vaguely worried, she kept at his heels nevertheless, trying to be helpful, chatting incessantly, giving him the story of

94

her life in little bursts and clutters, catching each and every one of the quick reassuring smiles he was flashing at her as a duck on a half-frozen pond would catch breadcrumbs thrown by a generous hand.

Together, they had erected the fallen fence and filled in the worst gap in the stone wall around the tiny front garden, so that when the cattle gathered around the *hafodty* again in the evening they would be kept at a reasonable distance.

At night, after they had eaten a meal together which Brett had cooked, and sat by the fire which Linda had built, she told him about the shadow, and about the hand on her shoulder that couldn't have been his, yet was.

'You've lived without a man for much too long,' he said mildly, but with a kind of authority that startled her, and she cried.

John Brett was not a pig of a man. He was, in fact, soft and tender and never in his life had he taken advantage of a woman. But there was something in those silent torrential tears and in the way Linda just let them fall, so that they drenched the shirt on her breasts, that brought on a warm compassion, a strong desire and lust he hadn't felt for ages.

He bent over, put his arms under her knees and shoulders and lifted her up. She helped him, she clasped her hands behind his neck and hoisted herself as much as she could, trying to hide her face in his beard. He sought her lips, but when he kissed her her response was so timorous and trusting that he nearly put her down again.

'Listen, honey,' he murmured, 'I don't want to mess you up.' But she shook her head vigorously, and clung to him, and he carried her into the room he knew she slept in.

Had somebody asked Linda what on earth she thought she was doing, she would probably have snapped out of this, made some intelligent excuse to Brett, and preserved the precarious balance of her life. But of course nobody did. Nobody's ever there when needed most.

She insisted on keeping her shirt on, and tried to cover as much of her body with it as she possibly could; until she forgot. She forgot everything, and for a moment she was painfully aware of the void she had become.

Luckily, there was no need for her to do anything; she wouldn't have known how. John Brett was a self-absorbed lover, quiet, slow, almost lazy. Yet he seemed to be listening for something, as he dwelled and waited. Surprised, Linda began to listen too – and there was, indeed, some kind of music, little percussion instruments were drumming up from within her own body, tiny muscles were twisting and dancing, and she just had to laugh with delight, it came out in a soft chortle, and that made her respond to Brett, who was listening, and all hell broke loose, hot and overwhelming.

At-the-age-of-forty-four!! She must have cried it out loud, because she heard him laugh too; for a second she felt nothing but ferocious wrath, and then it all ebbed away leaving but the sweetest imaginable little ripples.

You old fool, said a teeny voice. Poor Linda, said another, you silly wanton wretched Linda. You'll pay, said a third.

John Brett was accustomed to waking up early. He loved watching the darkness retreat, being pursued, and finally defeated, as if the assertion of light was, each morning, his own victory. He also loved the slow dawn of memory, first dimly entangled with dreams, then jostling them away and marking the day with the simple truth of yesterday.

He remembered Angharad first and thought that the purring of his body from head to foot was connected with her; it was a moment of great happiness and wonder. Then the image of Linda wedged in; her soft, slow burning body; her artless abandon; her astounding climax, the pain on her face. Wow.

Unless she was having me on, he thought suddenly and turned his head sharply to look at her – but she was not in bed with him.

96

She was easy enough to find, all huddled up in an armchair by the fireplace and surrounded by crumpled sheets of paper, but the shock of desertion, the threat of unreality, was too strong in him just to vanish. He carried her to bed rather roughly, threw her down and waited.

She muttered something, and slept on, like someone exhausted after a night of utter anguish.

For pity's sake! Brett covered her up, and went out.

White mist was sliding down the meadow, low above the ground but thick as cotton wool. Wading through the mist to the stream and back, Brett was but a powerful torso of a man with hips but no legs, arms but no hands, and the sense of unreality was turning his stomach. Magpies shouted abuse at him and two young bullocks stampeded away as if they'd seen a ghost. A huge cow stood on the top of the rocky hill, black as the devil himself, pushing against the milky sky, holding the sun back.

And yet it rose from behind the beast's backside, like a glorious shit. If Brett could stretch his neck out and bellow, he would have done.

'That fellow,' said mother, 'has he come to stay or what?'

'What fellow?' said Angharad coldly. 'Will you pass the butter, please, mother? Boys, if you don't stop kicking the table you'll go without breakfast. If your grandma's spoiling you, I won't.'

'What a shame for a big man like him not to have any home or family. Mooch round other people's land! What is the matter with him?'

Brett felt better after breakfast, but not particularly inclined to work. There was still no sign or sound from Linda; he lit a cigar and smoothed out the crumpled papers she had obviously spent the night with. Her handwriting was easy to read, it was a familiar cosmopolitan scrawl and gave him an absurd feel of, and longing for, New York.

Dear Alice,

Wish I could be with you right now – buried among those deadly green cushions on your sofa, peering through the combined exhausts of our fags, gulping down that dreadful Vodka Absolute – Remember the night – about a year ago – when Ruth gave us that long rambling lecture On Orgasm? You said she was being utterly ridiculous, I said she was a liar and a myth-maker, and she said you and I were a disgrace to modern femininity!

Well, I don't know –

Do you, by any chance, remember whether she mentioned a killer of a headache, brief but awfully punishing, right after the Ecstasy? Alice dearest, I am terrified, I am so unhappy, I was such a fool, but please don't laugh at me. And don't tell Ruth!!

There is no great mystery in this. I thought there was but – Anyway, he is a kind of a travelling repair-man, he takes on stray people and broken things, and I suppose I looked just like an old rusty toy of a woman breaking down – never really properly finished in the first place – so naturally he thought of mending me.

I could have done without the Experience! It's far too late in life – I feel I've lost something – I forbid you to laugh – some kind of virginity, you know what I mean! We prided ourselves on it often enough, you and I!

Why did I ever run? There I was in London, with a perfectly good friend and a half – I take you for an equivalent of ten friends, dear Alice, but then Ruth had the other eight and a half of you – and with everything going for me, why, I could have had meals on wheels, if I wanted to, and go to a singles' club, and have my hair done regularly by Unisex, and –

Oh Alice, I've virtually thrown myself at him! My skin feels funny too, I could pick it up at any spot and peel it off, maybe there is a new woman underneath –

Dear Ruth,

I tried to write to Alice about this, but somehow it didn't –

Dear John Brett,

I won't be here in the morning, so this just a brief Good Bye. I wish you a pleasant stay and please don't –

Dear Dr B.,

Wish you were near! Believe it or not, but I've just had a freak orgasmic experience – yes, here on the mountain! – the first in my life and possibly – hopefully – the last, and I am badly shaken. I've thrown myself at a complete stranger, a silent furry hulk of a man; you can imagine I've told him all about myself, I went right on blabbing and he didn't seem to be paying much attention, so in the end I howled, I really couldn't help myself, and he took pity on me. And then it was as if I've lost all memory, and I am scared – who says there is no life without memory, Marquez? One hundred years of solitude –

There is a question I'd like to –

Dearest John,

I've done something awful, I've been unfaithful to you, I've been so faint-hearted. I should have known it was your shadow, your hand! I should have known that you have not deserted me, that you couldn't have; it was you who was prompting my spirit and I was so blind!

Can I go to him and say – sorry, Brett, it was just a case of mistaken identity? But it may no longer be true, forgive me, my dearest. I went all the way to meet him, and I have never done that before, and it wasn't that I wanted to, or that he was trying to make me, it was a complete surprise and I shall not lie to you – it was wonderful. It was too wonderful to go entirely without pain, but that may be my particular problem, I always seem intent on punishment whenever something beautiful happens to me.

Like you – I've never had a more perfect lover, I've never been lonely with you, you've never crowded me, and what did I do? I let you go, just for the pain of it!

I know nothing about the man, my dearest, which is just as well I suppose, because –

He isn't you, is he, John?!?
There is such an awful howling wind outside –

Dear Honorah and Richard,
I would like to thank you for your generosity. I've had a most wonderful time up here, perhaps the most wonderful time of my life, certainly of the last five-odd years of it. I suppose all good things have to come to an end –
Mr Brett, you might be glad to hear, definitely lives up to his reputation, he has already fixed the roof and the rain spouts and some of the fences and walls, and he seems to be enjoying himself. I don't want to be in the way, and anyhow, I have to –

The last letter was addressed to 'Frantishka' and contained only a few words in a foreign language, presumably Czech. Reluctantly, Brett crumpled the seven sheets of paper again, and dropped them where he found them.

Linda was right, he was not paying much attention to her chatter yesterday. He was thinking of Angharad and the way she belonged, the way she was anchored in these tough little mountains, and proud of it. Angharad was a life-grower; Linda was merely another homeless drifter like himself.

Maybe the homeless were the salt of the earth: the sharpeners of senses, the conductors of messages, the grounders of thunderbolts; but Brett was sick and tired of it.

At least, he thought warmly, she was not having me on. His chest swelled. There was something immensely gratifying in being the first in a woman's life, even if she was a perplexing, and possibly quite mad, little stranger.

Linda slept through most of the morning, waving her arms and kicking her feet in a series of flying dreams. She hadn't had those for ages, and she was enjoying herself tremendously, until the very last moments before waking up. She flew into a church and was trapped. The air was thin and there were no currents to lift and carry her, she was flying very low, dragging her kicking feet above the heads of the congregation; anyone could have pulled her down. And she was practically naked! In mortal anguish and shame, she crashed through the nearest and tallest window, and slowly regained consciousness amidst floating splinters of glass as colourful and as soft as a hummingbird's feathers.

Finding herself in bed was a shock – she could have sworn that she had, must have, crept away in the night! She felt, on the whole, terribly sorry for herself: until the mirror told her that she had become overnight the handsomest woman on the whole mountain.

She found her silly unfinished letters on the floor in the sitting room, and kept blushing while burning them in the fireplace, realizing that Brett must have carried her heavy sleeping body to bed early in the morning. Had he, she wondered, noticed the change in her?

Brett was clearing out the old well; it took a lot of digging. She left him standing in the muddy hole and ran down to the village to get some fresh eggs, milk and bread. She was back in well under two hours, she nearly ran all the way up the path too, surrounded by a cloud of flies frenzied by the heat and her sweat. Her heart was pounding, her mouth was dry, and she was happy.

Some reversed magic was at work. There were milk, eggs, and a loaf of home-made bread already on the kitchen table.

'Angharad's been,' said Brett, sounding indifferent. He kissed Linda on the mouth, softly and tenderly, and returned to the well which was showing signs of resurrection.

After supper, he opened a large bottle of Canadian whisky intended as a present for the Owens which he in the end hadn't quite known how to make. It was a good whisky with a lovely smell: they fell to, and made a night of it.

It was Linda's turn to listen to the story of a life, and although Brett gave it to her in a much neater form than she had been able to give, she didn't pay much attention either. She could not entirely escape hearing it, and now and then she wished she could. But she enjoyed watching him: the flicker of the flames was most becomingly reflected in his amber eyes. Sometimes his whole head seemed to be on fire, and his body was big enough to fill an entire private universe.

John Brett, to start with, was an orphan. The old teacher and his wife with whom he lived as a boy in a small village near Halifax, Nova Scotia, spoke often of his father and agreed that he was as good a man as any, but disagreed about the manner of his death. The teacher said he went down with a US submarine during the war, while his wife maintained that he came back all right but was killed soon after in a train crash near Quebec, though what he was doing in those parts was a mystery. Neither of them ever mentioned a mother – and Linda was tremendously relieved, she had enough trouble with her own lively ghost of a mother in her dreams.

Brett, the teacher said over and over again to the boy, the most important thing in the life of a man is ambition. Consequently, John Brett never had any. He had to pretend though, for he loved the old man and did not want to hurt him. He went to Toronto on a scholarship, and graduated in theology and economics; then he moved over to New York and became a fashionably unsuccessful freelance journalist, in which guise he journeyed to Vietnam and eastern Europe. Then the 1960s were over, and Brett himself was over thirty and thoroughly fed up with the whole world of politics and broken hopes. The old teacher died at the age of ninety; Brett was on his way back to Toronto to get a teaching post at the university. He was enormously relieved that he could stop pretending now. Instead of going to the university, he went to his old teacher's grave and buried his diploma, his press pass and his American Express card in the freshly moulded earth, replaced the wilting chrysanthemums and walked off to become a farmer's hand in the upper regions of Nova Scotia, the land of lamb and cattle, short summers and long, long winters, and life so hard you could hear its knuckles crack.

He liked it, the life and the farm and the couple he worked for and their fat little children and the brave old pony he was given to ride. He liked the lambing and the haymaking and the shearing and the occasional dance. He earned little and spent less. He rode to church on Sundays, grew a beard and eventually married a girl called Margaret McLeod.

Miss McLeod came from a wealthy family. She herself had progressed from fashion modelling to founding a chain of soaringly prosperous vegetarian restaurants, had become rich in her own right, kept meeting the wrong men with the wrong ideas and finally, still in her twenties, got rid of them all, donated half her wealth to an Eskimo craft centre and bought a farm with the rest of the money. The farm was a mere fifteen miles from where Brett was working and he met her at a dance. She was beautiful, tall and strong.

Linda was too tipsy to mind. She had to go for a wee, though. Squatting under the stars, exposed to the furious wind, she felt some ancient sorrow entering her body and heart. What a waste to invest life in somebody like me, she told the dark, arched, coldly glittering heaven.

Anyway, continued John Brett hurriedly when she returned, it didn't last. Margaret was a generous woman and settled half of her property on her husband. Being a real farmer, a man trying to squeeze some profit out of his land and stock, was no fun for Brett. The whole area suddenly revealed itself to him for what it really was, a reactionary backwater in both human and political terms. Brett dug out his theology and economics but they were constantly interfering with each other. For a couple of years he and Margaret produced a monthly newsletter, *The Ram*, and tried to introduce some new ideas, stir up some sense of solidarity in the farming community; but the harder they tried, the fewer subscribers they had, until the whole thing folded up, and so did the marriage.

Margaret wanted children, as many as she could bear, but none came. It would have been all right perhaps if it were her fault, but it soon proved to be Brett's. His sperm count was so low that he was practically sterile – a true man without ambition. He stayed until the divorce came through and a new husband moved in, then he walked off with a rucksack on his back and snowshoes on his feet, humming a song and waving back until the farmhouse was out of sight. Margaret, with her usual generosity, had settled a good sum of money on him, but he had touched very little of it – it was still sitting in the bank.

He had walked ever since, up to Alaska and back to the lakes, taking up occasional jobs, learning new crafts and skills, forgetting all abstract knowledge, never setting foot in a church, bookshop, cinema, theatre or library.

What about women, Linda wanted to know. Whereupon he got up from his chair, patted her head awkwardly and hurried out. Linda fiddled with the fire and was bitter. At least, she thought, at least you don't have to squat, do you, or bare your bottom. You cut a proud figure standing there in the wind, gushing away. She remembered her grand-mother, the one who pissed like a horse, chuckled, and felt better.

She would have told him about her grandmother when he came back, but before she could open her mouth he was talking again. Did she know, he asked rhetorically, that he had been to Prague in 1968?

I am going to get drunk like a sailor, decided Linda, and then, perhaps, I won't mind whatever he says, or does. I am too old for this kind of life-swopping, fate-tempting, merging of destinies. And so is he!

'Maybe we've met, Linda. Hey, maybe we've really met before! Isn't it terrific?'

Of course we've met, she thought, listening to him going on and on; Prague was full of wild-eyed Western journalists in 1968. You had no beard then, your skin was smoother and the freckles weren't showing so much, and you were probably quite thin. I bet you wore a sky-blue denim suit, and leather-strap sandals without socks – until you bought a pair of blue-white tennis shoes, Czech-made and ridiculously cheap. All foreigners were buying them; Ben wouldn't wear anything else. I bet you carried a miniature camera in your pocket and a small, flat tape-recorder in your hand. I bet you came straight from Paris, from students' barricades, and found the Czech girls ever so much nicer. You sat on the grand staircase of the Rudolphinum concert hall, and strained your neck turning your head from right to left, from that magnificent panorama of Prague Castle up on the hill behind the river to the poster-plastered arcades of the philosophical faculty. I sat there through every lunch hour, scribbling the worst poems of my life on greasy paper bags; of course I must have met you. I bet you flashed a smile at me and said 'Dubček!' instead of 'Hello!' – and added a V-sign!

Brett, damn you, it's all over!

Look at yourself. Look at me!

Will you shut up, please, and carry me off to bed? One more night, and then I'll go.

But it was a large bottle, and they'd drunk too much already to stop. Brett was shouting. If he'd only stayed in Prague till August, he'd have shown the Russians what's what! What kind of people are you anyway, he demanded to know: why the hell didn't you bloody fight! By and by, Linda became aggressive too, and wanted to know whom did he think he was deceiving with all that faked innocence he was putting on. Dick and Honey, perhaps: they didn't know what cheating meant. Oh yes, he was a cheat all right; with all that money sitting in the bank, it was easy to bum around! God's simpleton, indeed; a graduate in theology! A New York journalist! I don't want to mess you up, Linda honey, he said: why then, pray, didn't he tell her who he was? She wouldn't have yielded to him like he was a godsend, she wouldn't have been such a holy cow herself!

Later on, they made up, and laughed a lot. He told her

he'd read her letters and thought she was pretty mad, but really rather formidable. She giggled and told him about Ruth and Alice, and about how the three of them tried to set up a lesbian *ménage à trois*, and failed miserably, not knowing exactly what one was supposed to do with another woman's body. She even told him about John! He nodded wisely, and then burst out laughing and admitted that he was given to a similar kind of daydreaming himself, more often than not, and far less innocently.

'Are you in love with Angharad?' asked Linda after she had lost all defences but, unluckily, before her tongue refused to move.

'You leave Angharad out of this,' said Brett, and it was as if he had spat at her, there was such scorn in his voice.

They made up once again, but there was a kind of dirtiness between them which neither of them liked. Brett wanted to know about Orgasm. Linda tried to oblige. He told her about Margaret and her techniques. She said he was a pig after all, and went out and was sick onto a cowpat under the oak tree and spent ages covering the mess first with handfuls of grass, then with the soil Brett had dug out from the well. She kept carrying it over in her cupped hands as if her life depended on it; in the end, she built quite a barrow, and wondered what or whom was buried underneath. There was plenty of sad, grey light: the day was about to break.

She found him asleep on the rug by the fireplace and sat by him mournfully until she, too, collapsed; she slept with her head on his thigh and had desperate dreams about earth crumbling under her feet, about crying for help and getting none.

The whisky was good. They both woke up fresh after only a few hours' sleep, with a mere hint of a headache, a complete and beneficial blackout of the previous night's events, and a pleasant feeling of complicity.

Happiness is so simple, thought Linda, kneeling on the brink of the old well and clearing away soil and dirt. There is nothing elaborate to be done with it, just breathe it in and out.

Brett was now up to his shoulders in the well; every five minutes Linda would lean forward and kiss him on the mouth, cheek, nose, hair, ear, neck or bare shoulder, whatever was easiest to reach when he straightened up to discard another shovel-load of earth. He had completely uncovered the ancient stonework of the well's walls; it was beautiful and touching and slightly forbidding, as if they were working their way into a long-lost world; the cold, bitter-sweet smell of the yet invisible water was intoxicating.

I love him, thought Linda. I love him; and it isn't because I know him, I love him; I loved him before he told me about himself; I loved him when I went to bed with him; I loved him the moment he came here; I loved him before he came; I loved him before his name was mentioned; I loved him when I first thought about love. When I was fifteen years old and sat on the warm granite of Stalin's left shoe with a slim book of poems in my lap and gazed across the river and the clutter of the Old Town into the faraway horizons and pondered Love, great Love, *l'amour fou*, I loved him. I was worried then, scared really, and I am scared now; but I am happy.

I have taken an awfully long time to grow up, she thought in a sudden grip of sadness, I have nearly lost myself in the process. . . . But I am happy now.

'Mother please, stop meddling!' Angharad sounded stern, trying to conceal how glad she was that her mother had suggested she should bring John Brett over for lunch or supper. The boys jumped at the idea; a farmer from Canada was an exciting person to meet, surely he would be just like the cowboys in the movies, lots more fun than anybody around here!

'Okay,' she said, 'I'll ask him, but see that you behave.'

Angharad had been a widow for three years, and although she had had offers, and her mother never stopped matchmaking, she did not take the idea of marrying again at all seriously. She liked being her own mistress, running the farm as well as, and maybe better than, any man.

John Brett looked like a man who would understand, and would not try to take over.

And he was the first man she had met who was noticeably taller than herself. A foolish thing to delight in, but she did. She wished that that woman Linda would go back where she belonged, and immediately she frowned. Angharad was a kind woman, and this was an unkind thought.

At noon, the burning sun and the whipping wind became unbearable. The sea far below gleamed like a hot melted alloy of gold and lead; everything else appeared blurred, as if the entire frustrated landscape were on the run. The cattle sought shelter in a narrow gorge between the forest and a group of rocks further down by the stream. Brett and Linda, waiting for the water to seep through the mud, persevered a little longer, but in the end they too gave up and went inside.

In the cottage, the air was cool and dark; the contrast soon made them shiver and they went to bed, taking their tea and sandwiches with them.

At the end of that intimate meal, Linda told Brett about her inability to share a bed.

'I'll teach you,' he offered, 'you really musn't do this to a man. We are a scary lot, didn't you know? Terribly insecure. I bloody nearly hated you when I found you sleeping in that chair. I had you in my arms when I fell asleep, and that's where I wanted you when I woke up!'

'I'll try,' she promised, blushing.

'You can start right now,' said Brett and yawned. 'Listen, honey, I hope I wasn't too crazy last night! I haven't done much talking lately, and I guess it just went to my head. Don't tell me you're not sleepy!'

'I am,' lied Linda.

With great care and a tenderness that was almost embarrassing, Brett settled her in his arms and by his side, sighed contentedly, and fell asleep.

The afternoon drifted along uneasily, feverishly. Tooth and nail, Linda was holding on to her happiness, defending it against old fears and new anxieties, pushing away an inexplicable panic her body seemed to be aching with, trying not to shiver, not to wake him up, wishing he would. Why she felt that they were running out of time, she did not know; yet every lost minute made her wince with pain.

Strange: the only thing that did not bother her, that did not seem to matter at all, was the certainty that he did not love her. Perhaps she was even glad he didn't; she could concentrate on loving him, on embracing him with her entire being, on herself being nothing but an uninterrupted flow of affection, passion, trust . . . and panic.

Wake up, John, please wake up, she pleaded, silently at first, then in a whisper.

He may have slept like a child, but he woke up like a man, fully aware of her presence, her body. Immediately, urgently, his hands sought her naked skin underneath her clothes, and he followed them with his mouth. Linda buried her fingers in his hair and let her body arch and yield and meet him, and not once did she try to escape a touch, a pleasure, or a desire for one.

Not once did she try to cover herself up again, to hide her wrinkles, folds, veins and scars. 'Bless you,' she whispered, and what she meant was thank you, thank you for sweeping away a lifetime of shame, guilt, disbelief and fear.

Not only did she keep her eyes open; she was actually looking, seeing. The straining tendons of his neck; the sinewy shoulders; the fury of the freckles and the red hair on his arms; the hairless creamy flesh in the small of his back between his T-shirt and his jeans. She put her hands there, and they became alive, independent, greedy. Even her toes twitched with delight and sought whatever they could reach of his bare skin – his toes, ankles, heels and soles. Brett giggled and she laughed and dug her fingernails into his back.

He loves me, she thought, he must do. I shall never let him go.

You old fool, said a teeny voice. Whom do you think you're kidding? said another. You'll pay, said a third.

And Brett was wishing he hadn't started this. He liked Linda much better the other night, when it was dark and she wasn't pushing herself, when she lay, subdued, in a soft glow of sadness and tranquillity, until he took her by surprise.

The strong afternoon light wasn't kind to her. Brett disengaged himself, kissed her on the nose and drew a blanket up to her neck.

'Keep warm,' he said, 'I'll be back.' He tugged his trousers up and tucked his shirt in as he went; his back was smarting and he pulled a face Linda was not meant to see.

She couldn't see it. She was looking at the ceiling watching a large hairy spider crossing it diagonally; it was moving swiftly and with a certain dark grace. Linda remembered an old superstition which she used to observe rather anxiously when she was young: see a spider in the morning – bad luck; at noon – love; in the evening – happiness.

Didn't it follow, then, that at this afternoon hour she was halfway between love and happiness? That she could have both?

Or neither, said a teeny voice.

Angharad was standing in the kitchen.

'I was looking for you,' she said quickly and a little breathlessly. 'I called out and I knocked but the blasted wind is making such a din, I suppose you didn't hear me. Where is Linda?'

'Taking a nap, I guess.'

'Oh, I thought she might have gone back to London.'

'Would you like a cup of tea?'

'No. No, thank you. I have come to fetch you, as a matter of fact. I mean everybody is dying to meet you, the boys and mother of course, and we thought – if you didn't mind – would you have supper with us tonight? I've got the truck up on the road. She is a bumpy old rattler, but you don't mind, do you? You could write her a note so that she is not

110

worried when she wakes up – Linda, I mean. So what do you say?'

'I'd be delighted,' said Brett and meant it. He had only one problem: it would look odd if he put on his wellingtons in this weather, and his only other shoes were in the bedroom, by Linda's bed. 'Listen, honey, why don't you go and have a look at the old well while I fetch my shoes and stuff? The water is still not coming through, but it's a beauty.'

'You are coming, then?'

'Sure I am.'

Angharad nodded and walked out and stood by the well, waiting. The mud on the bottom was full of bursting little blisters; there was no doubt that there was water underneath. Angharad felt her old impatience: why does everything take ages to happen?

Linda was awfully quiet while Brett was putting on his socks and shoes, and her eyes looked almost black.

'Listen, honey,' he muttered hastily. 'I know it's a bit of a mess. But I told her you were taking a nap, so she couldn't very well ask you, too, could she? I'll be back.'

'Sorry,' said Linda, 'I am a cow. I know you will. Have a really good time.'

But when he left, she drew the blanket over her face, pronouncing herself dead.

'You haven't noticed them eating thistles, have you?' Angharad was turning her head worriedly towards her cattle, huddled against the rocks below, as she and Brett were walking up the track, leaning and pushing against the wind.

Brett shook his head. 'There are still some good patches of pasture around,' he said, 'though not many.'

'If this dreadful weather stays on for another day, we shall have to let them into the forest, and never mind what the Forestry says,' decided Angharad, and whether or not she was aware of the 'we', Brett's heart warmed to it.

111

'There may be a storm tonight,' he said, thought briefly of Linda, and then not at all.

Linda was absolutely furious with herself. She jumped off the bed, grabbed a bucket full of water, ran outside and poured it all over herself. Drenched but still angry, she walked in the wind and gave herself a proper talking to.

Some love, she sneered, nothing but a snivelling self-pity. A grown-up woman, eh? Well, let me tell you that you had more dignity as a teenager than you're showing now. So he went to have supper with neighbours. So what.

So he is going to marry Angharad, that's what, said a voice.

And I knew it all along, said Linda, so what. What he gave me, what I took from him, what I virtually snatched from him, stole from him, was my own ability to love. I was like this weather, blowing myself to destruction, parched, choking in my own dust, trying to drink from a mirage, until he came.

He let me love him; he did not defend himself; why, he even helped me along! Nobody, but nobody, has done that for me, not since Frantishka was a baby and had not yet put up her defences too.

Brett chopped wood by the barn while the two boys were swinging on the gate, watching him. He loaded their arms with the sticks and marched them to the house. Angharad saw them from the kitchen window: they were flushed, gleaming, radiant.

'You'd better go and do something to your face,' said mother to Angharad, 'and your hair!'

Linda knelt down by the well, and gasped. Bubbling, spouting, springing and spurting, the water was coming through the mud, a tiny rainbow was arched above it, the air was dancing upwards and spraying her face with dew.

I give up, said the voice, and she was left in peace.

It was nearly sunset, and the wind had calmed down considerably; Linda sat by the well until it rose up again, this time with such a force that a buzzard was sent somersaulting across the sky and into the forest, followed by its shrieking mate. A thick branch broke off the oak tree and crashed down. In the east, yellow clouds began to flock and roll and heave, like poisonous smoke from some chemical plant. But the rest of the sky was as empty as ever. The sun went down and Linda fought her way through the gale to the cottage.

She had to bolt the door – the gale kept throwing it open otherwise. She shut and secured all the windows, yet they were still rattling incessantly and the *hafodty* was full of sudden draughts and alarming thuds and crashes and creaks.

Linda brewed herself a large pot of tea, abandoned all attempts to light a fire, sat down at the desk in her bedroom, and stared into nowhere in particular for a long while; by and by, she began to focus her gaze.

'I don't like this,' said mother. 'I don't like this at all. Come and look at the sky, John.'

Brett joined her by the window, and so did Angharad and the boys. The yellow clouds were a sickening sight.

'I'd better let the dogs into the house,' sighed Angharad. Brett went with her to the back door; the boys wanted to follow, but their grandma stopped them. The five dogs were already huddled against the door, whining anxiously, and were overjoyed to be let in.

Brett took Angharad's hands into his and kissed her, leaving a respectful distance between their bodies. Angharad nodded approvingly and smiled. As she was passing before him through the kitchen door, however, he could not resist patting her bottom. And that was okay with her too.

'Thank God we're all together under a solid roof,' said her mother and began ladling out the steaming soup. It was to be followed by a stuffed golden-brown chicken with plenty of the stuffing on the side, and three veg.

Linda was writing now, frowning most of the time. It was not a happy story but the one nearest to Brett, and one she would have skipped if they hadn't had that drunken night together and if he had not waved his fists against the imaginary Russians.

Chicken Boiled, Chicken Fried

The night before Warsaw Pact armies invaded Czechoslovakia, which means that it must have been 20 August 1968, Ben and Linda were having an unpleasant, teeth-gritting row. They'd had shouting matches before but this one was different, dry and hostile.

Hela had swooped on Ben that afternoon and, before he knew what had hit him, she had taken Frantishka away to her cottage in southern Bohemia. Linda came home in the evening and found him brooding. He did not like his child being kidnapped by that frustrated woman, he said; and no, dammit, he did not know when they'd be back, it was all so sudden that he had forgotten to ask.

Oh well, said Linda, the weather was nice and Frantishka could well do with country air and real fresh eggs. But that was not the point, shouted Ben in English as he always did when he was irritated, the point was that if Linda hadn't been such a lousy mother, so bleeding lazy, Hela could not have found it so damn' easy to step in whenever she bloody pleased.

If Ben wasn't a lazy father, retorted Linda, he would have taken Frantishka to some place in the country himself a month ago; it was easy for him to throw his stupid translations and his typewriter into the car and buzz off; she, Linda, had to go to work every day.

Work! sneered Ben. A bloody fête and a fancy dress party thrown together, more likely. Couldn't she get it into her fuzzy head that the whole democratic socialism bit would only bring the Russians in?

Nonsense! Linda flared up. They wouldn't dare! Anyway, that sounded great coming from Ben, him with his nose buried in the newspapers every morning and chuckling with delight whenever Dubček appeared on television!

He should never have married Linda, claimed Ben, very drily; they were too different politically. She was an incurable romantic; he was a pragmatist. Also, he was a family man while she was essentially a drifter.

Linda slammed the door on him.

In the morning the sky was heavy with military cargo planes and helicopters and the streets were full of Russian tanks, armour, and machine guns, manned by tired-looking, dirty, bewildered soldiers of the Red Army. Angry youngsters, empty-handed and hot-headed, were throwing themselves by the hundreds at each tank, old people were forming long silent queues in front of every grocery shop.

While Linda, choking with tears of anger and grief, sat paralysed with the fear that she might never see Frantishka again, Ben ran out and returned with a huge bunch of bananas. He'd grabbed it at a market stall before a queue shifted there from a nearby shop; they could survive on it for a week; or rather Linda could, because he, Ben, was going to try to get out of Prague, even if it meant driving the whole day through back alleys and forest tracks. He'd phone Linda in the evening, but should the lines be cut, she mustn't worry: he'd take care of Frantishka, he'd keep her out of harm, come what may. Linda should stay at home, because who knows, Hela might just be crazy enough to be on her way back to Prague right now, though he doubted it.

There were dark red blotches all over his face and neck, but he seemed calm and composed and Linda had never liked him better. Neither of them mentioned the row of the previous night; they embraced and kissed and looked into each other's eyes with all the affection there had ever been between them, and more.

Linda phoned the editorial offices of the literary review she worked at; no reply; she dialled all three numbers over and over again, but there was never any answer. None of her friends seemed to be at home, or had the whole town become deaf and dumb? Her mother, bless her heart, had answered the phone the third time Linda rang.

She had been out queuing, Emily said, but had given up. If this was the end, so be it. But frankly, she could not believe that the Russians would be worse than the Germans; and nobody starved to death then. There was a Russian tank at the High Street end of Quick Street; Emily had to walk by and mind you, it wasn't a nice feeling. The silly old Mr Beránek/Lamb shook fists at the soldiers, and one of them swung the machine gun towards him but straightened it out again when Emily shouted 'Niet, niet', which apart from da and spasibo were the only Russian words she knew. And she could have sworn that the other soldier by the gun, who really looked terribly young, was weeping. What a shame it all was, sighed Emily, and where was all that lilac blossom of 1945! He was playing a mouth organ then, said Linda, and tap dancing; Mr Beránek/Lamb that is. He was always silly, Emily concluded. But she would have to go now, Václav was getting terribly restless, poor old dear. He didn't know what was happening, of course; why, he didn't know what day and month it was; maybe he was the lucky one. He didn't have to watch the world go mad. Linda should stay at home and take good care of Frantishka, Emily said, and hung up.

Frantishka! But Linda was glad she hadn't told mother; why spread the anxiety? She couldn't remember when she dozed off, but she must have slept for hours, just like when she was little and things got too big to cope with. It was dark when the telephone finally rang: and it was Ben.

Everything was fine, he said, and sounded boisterous. Driving out of Prague was quite an adventure and he had nearly got himself killed, but he'd tell her all about it some other time. The important thing was that everything was peaceful and quiet in the village and, if it wouldn't have been for the wireless, people here wouldn't have noticed anything out of the ordinary. How on earth did the chaps in Prague manage to keep it operating even though the broadcasting house had been occupied by the Russians? Well done, and good for them, was all that Ben had to say to the radio chaps, and he did so in English. Frantishka was well and cheerful, by the way, and already brown like an Indian after only two days in the sun. And yes, he had taken his work with him, just like Linda had suggested, and Hela seemed pleased to have him there, so Linda oughtn't to expect them back in Prague sooner than in a week's time. Cheerio, he said, and would Linda take care of herself, and not let the bananas spoil. He already sounded like a man from another planet, or at least as if he had already gone back to England.

Linda tortured the telephone again, and this time finally got through to several of her friends at the same time, for they were all huddled together in one flat. They, too, sounded boisterous, all of them, though they were swearing solemnly that all they had had to drink was one bottle of rum among the six of them. Too bad Linda couldn't join them and bring another bottle or two or five, possibly; a curfew had been imposed and shots were heard from downtown.

What were they all so happy about, Linda wanted to know, Jesus Christ! Had she been to the streets, they asked. Well then, had she been – really! – she would have known that this was victory. Yes, victory! Where would she find them tomorrow, asked Linda anxiously, but they said they couldn't tell her on the phone, as they had all gone underground. She was one day late, but it was like being late a whole century, they claimed.

'You mean everybody's on their own,' whispered Linda, and once again, with that horrible twinge of pain, remembered her brother Jan. 'Oh no,' they all shouted into the phone. 'Oh no! Everybody is with everybody, nobody is on his own! She must go to the streets tomorrow – really! – and see the Asians choke on their own bile! They've never seen a free nation before!' Somebody said 'Hush!' and Linda said goodbye and hung up.

She cried herself to sleep and had idiotic dreams about frying lilac blossoms, peeling a mountain of bananas on a ship which seemed to be on fire, and teaching Frantishka how to crochet. Something she had never – really! – mastered herself.

They had been right though, her friends of yesterday. The

streets were wonderful, and it was victory. There was no government, no visible authority, only the wireless everybody kept listening to; transistor radios were willingly shared among many ears. An entire army had been immobilized, all that heavy shooting power was rendered useless, there was nobody to shoot at. Thousands were on the streets, each tank was surrounded by an angry, scornful, shouting crowd. But those people had no other weapons but words, and what army was ever trained to shoot at words? Young lives had been lost on the first day, mainly boys trying to set tanks on fire, but although every drop of their blood on the ground was covered in flowers, nobody was calling for blood in revenge.

'Go home,' Linda heard people yelling, and was soon shouting herself: 'Go home, idiots, don't you see you've been betrayed, fed lies, led into a battle where there is none, to combat a counter-revolution which never was?! Go home, for goodness' sake, leave us alone!'

A man with a child sitting on his shoulders pushed forward a woman with a baby screaming in her arms, so that she stood face to face with an officer sitting in a Red Army Jeep. 'This is my wife, savvy?' he shouted. 'Big Brother, these are my children! This is my city, my country, savvy? All I want is a decent life, a teeny weeny freedom to do as I please! So get the hell out of here!'

The baby kept screaming, the woman was crying, and the officer looked around desperately for help. 'What is he saying, somebody tell me what is he saying,' he repeated, and Linda, who couldn't stand it any more, translated the man's words into Russian. '*Gospodii pomeelooyi*,' moaned the officer, 'Lord have mercy!' He backed his Jeep a few yards and was out of it, for a while at least, but Linda was captured by the crowd and led from one encounter to another, and asked, commanded, to translate.

In the end there was no need to prompt her, to tell her what to say. She was quite intoxicated with her role of a spokeswoman, and was becoming bolder and bolder as they neared the very centre of the city. A bridge had to be crossed, though, and just then a platoon of Russian soldiers jumped off a lorry to carry out orders not to let anybody through.

'This is my city,' said Linda in Russian, 'my country. You have absolutely no right to order me, to order us, around. So get the hell out of here!'

The sergeant was tough: he commanded the platoon to put on bayonets. The crowd stepped back, but Linda, foolishly perhaps, did not. The point of a bayonet was pricking her stomach, but for the life of her she could not force herself to be frightened. The soldier behind the rifle had baby-blue eyes, they were enormous, and there was mortal anguish in them. She knew very well he would not, could not, drive the bayonet through her body.

The sergeant was too tough: he gave the 'Forward' command. The blue-eyed soldier threw his rifle down, and soon the entire demoralized platoon had to be ordered onto the lorry again and driven away. The bridge was free.

Linda, who had had nothing to eat since early morning, nearly fainted and was left in the care of the man with the two children and the weeping wife. They, too, were now feeling the strain. They had a thermos flask of hot cocoa with them, and a bag full of buttered rolls; they all sat down on the pavement and drank and ate the most bizarre picnic of Linda's life.

Later in the afternoon, while reading the countless – and mostly very witty – messages on home-made posters (like the one which said 'Lenin wake up, Brezhnev's gone mad!') plastered all along On-the-Moat Avenue in the heart of the city, Linda finally came across somebody she knew. The woman was Ben's friend rather than Linda's but still it was nice to talk to her. She was an interpreter by profession, a descendant of a White Russian family who had come to Prague in the 1920s, and she boasted at great length about how she had just refused an interpreter's job at the occupied town hall. She would not be seen talking to the bastards!

Linda, who was dreading going back to the empty flat, went to the town hall instead, and volunteered.

The mayor had gone underground and a deputy mayor was in charge, a skinny little man with a heart condition, a prewar education from Prague and Paris, and postwar re-education from Moscow; he was nobody's fool.

In charge of the town-hall-occupying forces was a handsome major who came from an old Russian family and looked like a character from Tolstoy's *War and Peace*; he was nobody's fool either.

Whatever kind of history was happening outside, sad, great, logical, or absurd, inside the town hall it was a mere tug of war, a black comedy, a costume farce.

The extras on the stage were some two hundred Russian soldiers standing, sitting, smoking, sleeping, eating on the cold ceramic-tiled floors of the public halls and corridors downstairs. And some dozen or so Czech clerks and councillors who felt enormously superior, not only because of their arguably superior cultural heritage, but also because they sat and slept on the sofas and on the soft thick carpets of the mayor's suite and other rooms upstairs.

It was the deputy mayor's major victory. He told Linda all about it the moment she was introduced to him, and touched upon the subject several times more during the long evening.

After the chaotic early morning hours of 21 August – what with the mayor going underground and the first deputy mayor going down with a sudden, life-endangering, summer influenza – he, the second deputy mayor had been found, brought in, and made to face the commanding officer of the town hall detachment of the Russian occupying forces, the handsome and painfully polite major.

The major complained that the old porter in the lodge had refused to surrender the keys of all such rooms in the building as were locked upon the detachment's arrival. It was a regrettable necessity that all such rooms were opened and searched for weapons of the counter-revolution, and eventually temporarily requisitioned for the purposes of the Red Army.

He, the deputy mayor, emboldened by the rather unbelievable fact that the keys had not been simply snatched from the lodge – the old porter could hardly have offered

120

any resistance – or the locks smashed or shot through, surrendered only the keys of the rooms downstairs and categorically refused to open the upstairs suites.

'Why?' asked the major.

He, the deputy mayor, said that those rooms contained antique furnishings, valuable pieces of art and expensive hand-made carpets, all gifts from, and the property of, the Czechoslovak people, and in particular the citizens of Prague.

'We are not here to steal,' said the major, and blushed crimson.

He, the deputy mayor, blushed too, but stood his ground. Perhaps not, he said, but an army detachment could not be expected to behave like a group of museum visitors, and incalculable damage would no doubt be inflicted on the furnishings, and the objects of art, all gifts from, and the property of. . . .

The major raised his arm and he, the deputy mayor, expected a blow. 'We are not pigs,' hissed the major through his teeth, turned on his heels and left the mayor's office followed by his two liaison officers.

It was at this moment that the deputy mayor in charge of the occupied town hall decided that he needed an interpreter. His Russian was adequate but not all that good, and a buffer between himself and the major was certainly needed.

Oh, and didn't he have an hour of sweat! A minute after the major left with the keys for the rooms downstairs, he, like the old fool of a deputy mayor he was, suddenly remembered that one of those rooms belonged to the town hall's division of the people's militia and would no doubt contain a cupboard or two of pistols and rifles, which would no doubt be interpreted as weapons of the counter-revolution; and he, the deputy mayor, would be shot.

He sweated for an hour, and then he couldn't stand it any more and sent the charwoman with her broom and dustpan downstairs on an intelligence mission. She was back in five minutes and reported that the people's militia club room had indeed been unlocked, but no one was in there and the cupboards were safely locked and untampered with.

121

'You and I, however, are sitting on a barrel of gunpowder in this very town hall, my dear,' concluded the second deputy mayor, and he opened a bottle of Stolichnaya, the very fine Russian vodka which is no longer freely available to ordinary citizens in the shops in Moscow.

The two hundred Russian soldiers in the cold halls and corridors downstairs were given a mug of tea and a packet of Russian cigarettes in the morning, and one meal a day. The grub, consisting solely of ugly-looking lumps of *kasha*, a kind of porridge, was delivered to them by Red Army supply trucks, and by the time it was ladled out onto their tin plates it was stone-cold.

'Mother should see me now,' Linda heard a young private sigh.

'Fuck your mother,' said his older mate, who was already dropping ash from his fast-burning cigarette onto the half-eaten *kasha*. 'I ask you,' he continued, 'is this the way to treat soldiers of the glorious Red Army? We are not pigs!'

The deputy mayor, Linda, the charwoman and the dozen or so clerks and councillors had their meals delivered on silver plates from the Pelican, one of the most expensive and celebrated restaurants in Prague, by waiters and cooks who were doing this as an expression of solidarity with the occupied town hall.

'Who is paying for this?' asked Linda after she discovered that caviare was included in almost every hors d'oeuvre.

'History,' I suppose, said the deputy mayor and shrugged his shoulders.

'Which means we all do,' said the charwoman, 'doesn't it?'

Not once were the enticing and fully laden trays requisitioned by the hungry soldiers.

There had been a heated discussion in the mayor's office about whether the major should be invited for at least one

122

lunch or supper. The question was voted on and, although the vote went strongly against an invitation, the deputy mayor asked the major nevertheless – for supper, which was usually less crowded as most of the clerks had gone home. The major came, accepted a glass of vodka, took one look at the dishes, blushed crimson, clicked his heels and left.

Various incidents were being reported to the town hall, by telephone or via the Russian liaison officers. Most of the reports concerned strange nightly shootings in the centre of the city. There were no casualties, indeed it seemed that the Russians were firing into the blue, although the liaison officers kept reporting it as 'retaliatory shooting by the Red Army at pockets of counter-revolution'. There was something ominous about this. The major was called and asked for an explanation. He offered none.

There was the tragic incident of a young woman shot and badly wounded on Klárov, a pleasant little square by the river. Apparently she was running to catch a tram, and a Russian soldier patrolling the square shot her in the back with his automatic rifle. He then collapsed himself and was last seen being shoved into a Red Army ambulance.

The major denied the incident strongly, and in his most official voice. No such soldier existed in the Red Army, he said. But when he met Linda later on in the corridor, he stopped her and spoke to her in his usual quiet, strained voice. 'You are a young woman,' he told her, 'you ought to be able to understand what is going on in our soldiers' minds. Such a lovely city, so many pretty girls; and all they get is hatred.' He did not wait for any reply, turned sharply and marched away.

'Go home, for God's sake,' called Linda after him, 'for the sake of all of us, go back to Russia!'

However hard she tried, and she did try, Linda could not feel any hatred. She was racked by a constant feeling of irretrievable loss; this wasn't politics, this wasn't even a war; this was some horrible mess, something had been done to life itself, something terribly shaming, like cutting off a limb, or a nose, or exposing a beating heart and then watching ugly scar-tissue grow over it. We've all died a little, the citizens of Prague and the soldiers of the Red Army; all of us. The soldiers knew it first, Linda supposed; the citizens protected themselves by defiance, but it was quickly degenerating into a pure racist hatred against everything Russian.

All things considered, Linda could find it in her heart to hate Leonid Brezhnev and all those comrades on the Politburo of the Soviet communist party who had voted for the invasion. But how could she hate the Russian conscripts? Weren't they all like her brother Jan? The major, of course, was a different matter, but he was hard to hate too; and he certainly was not an Asiatic barbarian.

But Linda's griefs and injuries were nothing compared with what the deputy mayor was going through. Each night he drank a bottle and a half of the fine vodka, in spite of his heart condition. He was challenging Death: come and get me, I am a mere wreck of a man anyway. He raged and pleaded and wept. 'I am a communist,' he cried, 'I've loved the Soviets, I've loved the Russians, and look what they've done to me, to my country, to my city, to my town hall!

'I believe in communism,' he pleaded, 'that can't be wrong, can it? It's a dream, isn't it? The best dream mankind ever had, isn't it?

'They've messed it up,' he wept. 'They've pissed on it and shat on it and dragged it through the mud.

'Who's they?' he shouted. 'I am the guilty one, there is blood on my hands! Why don't you spit on me?'

But he always ended up singing Russian songs, or rather bits and pieces which he could recollect, like the last lines of 'Moscow Fires', or the beginning of 'Far Away, Far Away', or the refrain of 'Commander Chapayev'.

To Linda's surprise, the charwoman didn't mind cleaning up the mess every morning. She liked the second deputy mayor best of the whole lot, the mayor included. Her husband had died a year after he had returned home from a German concentration camp; and that's where the deputy mayor had been during the war, did Linda know? That's why he was so skinny; some of them never recovered properly. And nervous! Why, he sometimes wept like a child, and his hands were shaking something awful. No wonder he drank. No wonder he messed things up. But he'd always been kind to her, and friendly, unlike some of the comrades she could name but would not, for peace's sake.

On the fifth morning, another tragic incident was reported. Four men had died the previous night as they were driving in a car past the main water supply plant in the southern suburbs of Prague and came under Russian machine-gun fire. The major had no explanation for the killings, but had not denied the incident.

The deputy mayor was summoned to the Soviet Command which had its headquarters in a school in the fourth district of Prague; he tried to procrastinate but was led out of the town hall at gunpoint and huddled into a Jeep flanked by two armoured vehicles. Linda was with him, for – as the major said – although they had their own military interpreter at the Command, his Czech wasn't very good.

The drive through the city was awful. Both the deputy mayor and Linda were painfully aware of people staring at them, thinking they were Russians or, much worse, collaborators!

An old general deputizing for the commander-in-chief, General Velichko – a deputy matching a deputy – read out a statement that the four men who died had clearly intended to sabotage the city's water supply, and that only the readiness and swift action of the Red Army had prevented a major disaster. The deputy mayor was asked to sign the statement, which also included a warning to the citizens of Prague that all acts of sabotage would be met with the same alacrity.

His hands shaking, and his voice quavering so much that Linda had trouble understanding him, the deputy mayor made the bravest speech of his life. He would not sign such a preposterous statement even if it should cost him his life. Why – according to the Czech police investigation, the car with the four men had not entered the water-plant premises but kept to the main road, and was not even slowing down when it came under fire; no warning was given by the Red Army unit. He, the deputy mayor, was responsible to the people of Prague, and for them, and he would never authorize this or any further murders under the pretext of sabotage. The only way how to end this ... this mess, was for the Red Army to realize that they were making war on unarmed civilians who were not a threat to anybody, and go back to the Soviet Union. 'For pity's sake,' he said to Linda in an exhausted whisper, 'tell them to get their bloody arses out of here.' She translated this in slightly more appropriate terms – the situation was nasty enough, they were surrounded and stared at by more and more icy-looking younger officers who were coming into the room.

But in the end, quite abruptly, they were allowed to leave, and to their great relief were not offered military transport back to the town hall.

The deputy mayor was rapidly breaking down; he looked old and frail and almost demented. Linda hailed a car down, and when she explained who the old man was and what he'd just done the driver willingly took them across the town to Linda's apartment and refused any remuneration. 'One for all, all for one,' he said.

The streets were changing, though. There were still posters on the walls and groups of people distributing leaflets or just standing together, but nobody was talking to the Russian soldiers any more. The original occupying troops were being rapidly replaced by new detachments, and those were no longer bewildered, shaken or demoralized. They came into an established situation and – as the Czech wireless still operating from various hideouts had warned – were dangerous and trigger-happy.

Linda put the deputy mayor to bed; he fell asleep instantly, his eyelids twitching like a bird's. After she had phoned the town hall and announced sternly that no, he would not be back until next morning, he had done his bit and wasn't it somebody else's turn now, Linda had a luxurious, long-needed and well-deserved bath and a change of clothes. She put her old clothes straight into the washing machine; they reeked of cigarettes, sweat and all the dirt of the tortured town.

In the evening Linda made a potato goulash and opened a bottle of cheap Czech rum – a welcome change from the Pelican cuisine and town hall cellars. The deputy mayor sat silently through most of the evening; then he wanted to know, if Linda was proud of him. Of course she had been – she still was, she assured him.

Well, he was not proud of himself, he said tearfully, it was all too easy and all too late. Did Linda know that his late wife, Olga, may she rest in peace, was Russian? They had fallen in love when he was studying in Moscow in the 1950s, and it was awfully difficult to get a marriage licence, such marriages were not encouraged. He had bribed the system, in kind . . . nothing Linda would like to hear about . . . dammit, he practically sent a Russian friend, Piotr, into a labour camp in Siberia! Olga was never really happy in Prague, although she very much wanted to come; maybe she finally died of homesickness, nothing else seemed to have been wrong with her. I loved her, he wept, I've loved the Russians!

Linda felt queasy, yet she pitied the man, and all of his kind: such warped lives! And she was violently glad that she had never been a party member, that she'd never become a communist, that she had had it out like tonsils by the time she was fifteen!

Democratic socialism! With these people sitting in the town halls, holding every chair? And as the charwoman said, the poor deputy mayor was perhaps the best of the lot!

Linda forced herself not to think politics any more; she was far too tipsy for that. The rum was gone, they were drinking bottled beer now. I'll teach you a song, said Linda all of a sudden, a Russian song! It's a street song, and it's simple: you'll learn it in no time. Half an hour later, the two of them were singing it to perfection:

Boiled chicken, fried chicken,
But chicken also wants to live!

They've captured it,
They've arrested it,
Where's your passport? – come on, give.
Don't you burn me, don't you shoot me,
I'm no Soviet, no fascist!
I'm your chicken,
I'm your darlin',
I'm the blackest anarchist!

When they arrived at the town hall next day, the old porter motioned to them to join him in the lodge. Dubček was speaking on the radio. He and the other members of the Czech Politburo, kidnapped to Moscow on the first morning of the invasion, had returned to Prague. Everything's going to be all right, he seemed to be saying, the government is being restored to its proper functions right now, the party will continue its course of democratic reforms we've pledged ourselves to. . . . The protocol we've signed in Moscow means only that the Soviet troops will be stationed in our country for a limited period of time, temporarily. . . .

But Dubček's voice was the voice of a broken man. There were audible sobs and tears in it, the words were trailing into long silences; it spelled ca-pi-tu-la-tion.

Linda had spent most of her pity on the old deputy mayor, now she was becoming numb. Sad perhaps, but numb. She pitied Dubček only very briefly, and went upstairs to collect her notebooks and spare knickers.

The Red Army detachment was clearing out. The major came to say a brief goodbye. 'All the best, Lindotchka,' he said, 'cheer up.'

Lindotchka my foot, a little childhood voice sang up in Linda, *shokolat, hollandskyi!*

The office workers were coming in, the mayor was expected any minute, there was no longer any need for him to stay underground. There was no longer any need for Linda's services, either.

The deputy mayor clutched her hand like a frightened boy. 'They'll soon have me for what I did yesterday,' he whispered, 'you'll see. I'll be done for it.'

A year later almost to the day Linda, passing by the town hall, stopped in her tracks and contemplated the familiar façade. She had plenty of time, she was freshly unemployed: the literary review she worked for had been closed as one of the first casualties in the general clampdown on the country's cultural and academic institutions, the 'instigators of counter-revolutionary ideas'. Should she, should she not? In the end, she mounted the staircase and entered the vestibule.

The old porter drew her into the lodge. He wouldn't go upstairs, if he were Linda, he said. She had been talked about at a recent meeting, it'd been hinted that she had encouraged the second deputy mayor, maybe even misled him, over that water plant affair. It hadn't helped the deputy much, though: he'd been stripped of his party membership, and sacked, and found dead in his office, on the same day. The old heart condition. . . .

It was one of those freak days of reckoning, when things pile up on one another until the victim is left devastated and perhaps ready for a new beginning.

Linda went straight home from the town hall; she felt that she urgently needed an afternoon nap. At first she thought that Ben had taken Frantishka to the park, but the apartment felt strange, far too empty. On the kitchen table she found a note saying that Ben and Frantishka had gone to England and would not be coming back. 'Sorry, Linda,' Ben wrote, 'but I had to take the car. Frantishka didn't want to leave any of her toys behind, not even her bike, and what with all the other things we could not very well fly. I can't let the child rot in this country! If you want a divorce, that's fine with me, but you will not get her back in Czechoslovakia. So come and join us.'

Linda phoned her mother, but Emily wasn't very sympathetic. Linda shouldn't have married a foreigner in the first place, Emily had warned her a thousand times. 'Now go, and bring the child back!' commanded Emily, and hung up.

Hela came over, stuffed Linda full of sleeping pills and left. She had an important editorial meeting to attend.

Socialist Woman was to expand; with so many other magazines being abolished there was more money, more paper and more printing capacity available, though with all the purges going on, staff could be a problem.

Linda slept like a dead woman; no dreams at all.

Later in the evening she was on the phone again. She was lucky with the third number she dialled. Grab a cab, she was told, and bring a bottle, will you? We're running out.

They were all there, her friends of yesterday, and they were all telling her not to be an idiot. Ben was right, of course, and as for Linda – oh boy, what luck! What a chance! What a privilege to be married to a Brit. at times like these! Just go, you silly goose, go, and don't you dare come back until this nightmare is over.

The combination of the day's events, the sleeping pills and the booze soon proved disastrous. Linda started to tell them about the deputy mayor, got all tangled up in the story, and was getting some pretty hostile looks from her friends. In a desperate attempt to make some sense, and to break the hostility, she took a guitar off a hook on the wall, sang 'Boiled Chicken, Fried Chicken' to them, and got herself thrown out of the flat, quite unceremoniously.

Russian songs of whatever kind, Russian language as such, were not permitted in any decent company.

A couple of months later Emily died, and Václav. Linda saw her sister for the last time, and left the country.

For ten years in England, she was as happy as Punch. She had a good job at the university, and lived the life of any other woman of her generation and similar profession; she worked, went to parties, had a mild divorce and a single child to bring up, tended mildly to the left, and read the *Guardian*. She found Ruth and Alice and moved in with them, they had lots of fun and lots of arguments they thought meaningful, and only a very few fights. She signed herself Linda Wren, and in some aspects became more English than the English.

She hardly ever looked back, consciously that is – she knew she mustn't! – and she would have lived happily ever after, if her mother hadn't taken over her dreams.

Linda could blame much on her mother; she blamed Emily for dragging her into the realm of unfulfilled, sacrificed, lovable perhaps but unloving, suffering women; and back into the suffocated land of her ancestors. Linda would suppress the dreams every morning, but they would be back at night, until eventually she ceased to know who she really was.

But Emily was not the only torturer; and she was, poor soul, a mere ghost. Linda's six closest friends of yesterday – that yesterday she would have either wanted to live forever or forever forget – took revenge on her, a bizarre, crucifying revenge.

They were scattered, and could easily have drowned in the sea of private bitterness, collective indifference and reckless materialism that swept the occupied country. But they did not. They reassembled and emerged among the several hundreds of the country's new elite, known as Charter 77, or the Chartists. A strange, natural elite, pushing through like tulips or irises which spring up in the middle of a barren field after years of waste, to remind everyone that there was once a garden underneath the arid soil, a supply of dormant bulbs. An impoverished and persecuted elite, anxiously clinging to the flagpole of morality and civil liberties. Subjected to unspeakable humiliation by the worst breed of state security agents, yet proud as the Czech devil himself.

Linda was torn between jealousy and admiration, thoughts of getting herself back to Prague, and the realization that she'd only be another century late. Why was she always, always, late for everything?!

By the time Linda Wren was forty, every single one of her six closest friends from Prague was in jail. Linda felt sick, horribly inadequate and a bit of a carrion-feeder when she collected a cheque for an article she had written about them for the *New Statesman*, a passionate, glorifying affair, and quite toothless. Sending the money to Prague helped only a little; she sobbed her heart out at Ruth and Alice.

'For Christ's sake,' they said more or less in unison, 'stop blubbing! It's happening to people all around the world, and much worse. We are all inadequate. Maybe we are all jealous of those who suffer, and maybe we actually dislike them, for the same reason: they seem to have a meaning to their lives. While we just carry on, and feel vaguely responsible for them. You're worse, you're sentimental, you're claiming some of the suffering for yourself, as if you had more right to it than we do.'

'I,' said Ruth, 'I had a very dear friend in Chile. He was killed.'

Alice spun around furiously. 'I have a brother in Manchester with three kids and a nagging wife. He's been unemployed for two years now. I can't talk to him! We've always been close. Now we hate each other's guts. There is a bleeding Persian Gulf between us. He says I'll never understand what it's like. He is right.'

'So what do we do?' moaned Ruth.

'How do I know?' growled Alice. 'Everybody's on their own.'

At the age of forty-four, Linda Wren was a wreck. She had nothing to lose, so she decided to fight her ghosts, and went to a lonely Welsh mountain to do so.

Boiled chicken, fried chicken, but chicken also wants to live!

When Linda finished the story, her eyes were so tired she could see nothing but an indiscriminate yellow light. Sunshine already?

Brett hadn't come back but she was not really expecting him to do so, it was only logical that he would stay the night at the farm. He'd be back; and she was looking forward to it. She wanted him to read this, and all the other stories she had written before, and the letters to John: she wanted John

Brett to know her. She had a grateful little thought: how nice that Ben's name wasn't John.

She went to the kitchen to make herself an umpteenth cup of tea, and then for the first time she realized that something was wrong. There was an absolute, huge silence, no gale, no birdsong, no nothing. The muscles of her stomach clenched. Unwillingly she went outside.

The yellow light was not sunshine. The sky was sunless, moonless, starless; where was the light coming from? She ran back and checked the clock: it was five in the morning, the time for a gentle blue dawn! Brett, please, she pleaded, come back soon!

She dragged her feet to Stalin's shoe: the whole world was yellow and silent. Even the black cattle looked a mere sickly brown as they galloped towards Linda, and the sound of their hooves was muffled as if they were running through a foot-deep layer of dust, and not stamping on parched fields and rocks.

Within a minute, Linda was hemmed in by the herd. But they meant no harm, they were as frightened as she was. Big beasts that they were, they came to her for reassurance, for help! Whatever it was that was coming, it would come from the sea, for it was there that the horizon was beginning to boil.

And if it was coming from the sea, then the safest place for the cattle would be behind the *hafodty*. The thick walls built from solid rocks were likely to withstand anything, and should the roof be blown off it would probably crash to the ground further away. The cattle gave her no trouble; they let themselves be led like the gentlest of lambs. And they seemed to agree with Linda's judgement, for they immediately lay down huddled together, and pressed their sides against the *hafodty*'s back wall.

'Bless you,' said Linda, and went back to the rock.

The slopes further down the valley were busy now. Men and their dogs were driving flocks of sheep off the wide open slopes and into the gorges at the bottom of the valley. There was probably lots of yelling and barking and bleating down there, but nothing penetrated the layers of deafness that engulfed the mountain. Without the sound, it looked quite funny, all those tiny figures running and flocking and disappearing. Linda giggled and sat down on the rock, drawing her knees up to her chin, making herself as small as possible.

Maybe that's it, she thought suddenly, maybe nothing is really happening in this world, maybe the yellow threat belongs to the world of my childhood? Maybe she was not meant to come out alive from the Tree Park when the whirlwind was crushing its trees forty years ago. Maybe she hadn't come out alive, maybe she died then, and was resurrected for a few brief months on a mountain to dream out a life . . . a life that wasn't all that much worth living. She had been a wild untamed child, a happy savage, unaware of being a female, untouched by either love or sorrow, crouching under her oak tree, playing with her poppy-queens; maybe she ought to have stopped right there; maybe she did.

But then, who was John Brett? Where did he come from?

The yellowness wallowing over the sea began to tear itself loose. Long tresses of cloud flickered upwards like the tongues of huge lizards. They too were yellow, only paler, much paler than the rest of the sky. The silence grew so intense that it hurt Linda's ears. The peak of Y-Wyddfa was being pushed further and further off, away into oblivion.

Linda looked back over her shoulder and sighed with relief. Both Moelwyns stood firmly and hugely in their places like two giants bracing themselves for a fight. Angharad's farm was somewhere behind them; tucked safely away as it were, should this really be coming from the sea, should it concern others and not Linda alone.

Don't come back, Brett, Linda pleaded, please stay where you are. You are safe. I am on my own. I love you – bless you, but I am happy on my own.

Angharad was smiling in her sleep. She and Brett had stayed up late the previous night, first watching the weather and then, when the gale had calmed down, talking and walking. Hinting at plans they could make together, holding hands, nothing more. The beauty of it was that he seemed to need her even more than she needed him, he was such a lost soul. And it was nice to know that he had his own money, there needn't be any quibbles between them over cash. She slept peacefully on, and did not hear the dogs whining again in the kitchen.

Brett did, and came down from the spare bedroom to let them out. The sky sure looked queer but apart from that everything seemed calm, dead calm.

He went to the henhouse to look for eggs. Happier than he had ever been, he thought of Angharad's warm, equable voice as she told him about the farm, and her late husband, and the boys; about her involvement with the Labour party; and about the love spoons her brother who lived in Cwm Croesor made during the winter months. She showed him a couple. They were beautifully carved and Brett was looking forward to making some himself when the winter came.

Had anybody mentioned Linda he might, he really might, have asked – and who is she?

The entire southern sky was now full of shooting tongues. It was quite beautiful to look at, quite like the *aurora australis* Linda had never seen, and never would see.

'Fiddlesticks,' whispered Linda, 'there is no limit to the things I shall see, now that I am on my own, free at last.'

'The ghosts are gone!' she shouted, and never mind that her voice fell flat on the ground.

I am in love with myself!

A blackbird ran past Linda's feet and kept running, down between the rocks and across the meadow towards the forest, pushed and wriggled through the moorgrass and the thickets of foxgloves, hopped down the bank and reappeared on the other side of the stream, still running, never flying, never taking to the yellow air. It ran past the stone wall, found

135

the gate, squeezed through the meshed wire and disappeared in the scrub at the foot of the pine trees.

So that's where all the birds are, thought Linda, sitting in their hundreds on the forest floor cushioned by layers of rusty needles. Hiding in that dark and impenetrable space under scruffy pines planted by idiots so densely that they suffocate each other.

It would seem now, she smiled, that there is a meaning to everything. Such a forest can hardly be uprooted. The birds are fairly safe.

All her instincts for survival were now tugging at Linda's muscles and joints, but she would not budge. I want to see what's coming, she argued, and I want it to see me. I am a good sight to behold. I am a part of this universe and, moreover, there is a good chance that I have actually created it. If I did, where would I hide?

The sea below looked like whipped cream, the silence was breaking. The sounds were small, like dogs whining in the distance.

Linda's stomach turned and her legs wanted to run, but her knees were locked firmly in her arms and she could not move if she wanted to.

She was scared now, but she was still arguing her case. I have created a man, haven't I? I borrowed a little, like people used to borrow a lump of yeast to start their own. I've created an image, and I loved it and abused it until it turned to flesh. Or until, more likely, it lured a living man into my lair. I loved him too, he may even think I abused him, but I haven't, I've let him go, haven't I? I have simply become a loving woman, for my own sake.

And now, decided Linda, I want to go and see my daughter. And Ruth, and Alice. And Dick, and Honey, to thank them.

But she couldn't wiggle a toe.

In a gigantic jerk, the long tresses of cloud tore off the horizon, surged to the zenith in one wriggling mass, and began to whirl and spin, faster and faster, shaped themselves into a perfect funnel and reached for the ground.

The leg of sky! Stamping, whipping, burning, swishing, whizzing, roaring. The yellow spell broke, and Linda ran. 'Join the cattle,' she shouted at herself, 'join the cattle!'

She was lifted off the ground and tossed high, and higher still, she was mounting the inside of the funnel, giddy but conscious, even registering brief little thoughts, like 'Ben was right, I am – essentially – a drifter', or 'Who says big women don't fly', and giggling. She missed the breaking tree tops by inches, but a flying branch hit her behind the ear; she was floating in a small cloud of blood now and the last thing she saw was the roof of the *hafodty* opening up like a cardboard box lid. Nobody's going to read what I wrote, she thought and was glad, glad, glad, and gave in to the roaring nothingness.

She was not to be granted such a lovely death. Together with a whole young birch tree that must have been uprooted further down the valley, and a tangled mass of bedding from the *hafodty*'s upstairs bedrooms, she was deposited in the uppermost corner of the meadow some quarter of a mile above the *hafodty*, as the whirlwind hit the steeper hills and began to break.

A shower of bricks from the chimney came down in the same spot, but Linda was hit by only a few, and the impact wasn't too bad as she lay under half a mattress and lots of foliage. She had broken a few bones, and there was the open wound behind her ear and another on her hip, but although she did not know it yet, she was alive and far from dying, provided she was found in time.

She was missing quite a spectacle. The yellow air was pushed out by blue-black, heavy, healthy-looking clouds that rolled in from the sea. The *hafodty* was on fire; a torn electric wire must have sparked it off. The flames were blazing up high but the solid outside walls stood intact, holding the fire in; it looked like a huge ceramic bowl in which an offering to the gods was being burned. The surrounding trees had all been crushed or uprooted and they lay strewn around the cottage like a green wreath. Gushes from the broken whirlwind were whizzing high above, just touching the tops of the flames, and a few sparks fell onto the parched grass, starting little fires. Most of these were stamped out by the cattle, who were careering up and down the meadow lowing and mooing in a frenzy of life.

Only the white cow lay dead by the stream, though she had no visible injuries; she must have been singled out for being different. Flocks of birds, large and small, were coming up from the forest as if flushed; they fluttered briefly above the pine tops and fell in again, screaming, hooting, whistling.

Then, just as a tuft of moorgrass caught fire and it was beginning to spread, lightning flashed, everything went white for one second and black for the next, and amidst the booming thunder water came pouring down from the sky.

Minutes later, when the thunderstorm had raged itself out and the downpour turned into a steady regular rain, all fires and flames were quenched and life went eagerly on.

Linda came to, and screamed, the pain was excruciating but it was also ugly, nauseating, humiliating. It was like being thrashed by some enormous perverted hands without knowing to whom they belonged, and where was this happening, and why.

She fought to make herself faint and nearly succeeded, but was licked back to consciousness by the rough tongue of a cow. The sight of the black beast brought her memory back, and once she knew who she was she no longer felt humiliated and was able to accommodate the pain, to make it bearable by relaxing her muscles and switching her attention from one ache to another, keeping them single and separate and trying to find out the reason behind each of them.

The roar of the whirlwind was heard many miles away. It had reassembled itself in the saddle between the two Moelwyns but that's where it died, too, throwing clouds of dust, grass and crushed slate over their tops in the process.

When the rain reached Angharad's farm the boys were screaming with delight as it was raining funny things, foxgloves and rags and sheep's wool and tiny shells, even a lampshade.

Brett was running down the track but Angharad walked; she had to drag herself forward. Lord, let them be alive, she prayed, and meant both her cattle and Linda, but Linda more, much more. It would be nobody's fault if the woman was dead, but it would be the kind of tragedy that leaves a shadow forever.

Brett shouted and yelled and, although she could not understand a word, something in his voice told her that all was well and she broke into a run.

'Hi, stranger,' whispered Linda, 'nice to have you around.'

'And you,' said Brett, truthfully.

'Bring them down!' he shouted at Angharad, pointing to the sky where an RAF helicopter glistened in the rain.

Angharad took off her yellow oilskin and flagged and waved it until it was clear that she had been spotted; the helicopter hovered and jerked as the pilot looked for a place to land. Brett had cleared the debris away and was holding Linda's hand; there didn't seem to be much else of her body that it would be safe to touch, but her eyes were bright and she was breathing, even talking.

'Anything I can do, John?' asked Angharad and he shook his head and gave her the most beautiful smile she had ever seen in her life. Her heart full to the brim, she wandered off to where her white cow lay dead by the gaily cascading stream.

She thought of the nice pattern the white cow used to make while moving backwards and forwards amongst the ebony-black herd and wished the helicopter would not take such ages to land.

'You are going to marry her,' whispered Linda and wanted to smile, but a pain shot through her head and she winced instead.

Brett shifted his weight uneasily. 'Listen, honey, I'm sorry if I messed you up a bit. We were both just lonely, I guess. Forget and forgive, will you?'

His hair and beard were darkened by the rain and the shirt clung to the flesh of his chest and stomach: he really looked rather like a big fat seal. This time, Linda managed a smile and kept it on until she was seized by a painful little cough.

'Hey!' shouted Brett. 'Hang on, honey! You'll come to the wedding yet!'

'I do love you,' he murmured hurriedly close to her ear, 'I always will. Just hang on there, come on!'

How do you tell a man, thought Linda drifting into a cosy faint, that he is not wanted any more?

Once the helicopter had landed it was a swift operation. The men had Linda strapped to a stretcher and tucked in a thermo-sheet in no time.

'Nasty freak of weather, wasn't it, sir?' said a young chap to Brett. 'Cigarette?'

'Is the lady family? Or a friend of yours?' asked the pilot.

'An acquaintance,' John Brett and Angharad said in unison, loud and clear, and embraced each other's shoulders as if they wanted to present a united front. The only particulars they could give were the lady's first name and the address of Richard and Honorah Owen, the unfortunate owners of the cottage and the lady's friends.

They walked the men and the stretcher to the aircraft and shook hands with everybody apart from Linda, who looked dead but was not.

'I don't know if it's any use,' ventured Brett, blushing perceptibly, 'but I happen to know that she is forty-four years old, and Czech. A British subject, mind you, but of Czech origin.'

'Thank you, sir,' said the pilot politely. 'I am sure the doctors will make some use of the information.'

And that's how it happened that everybody in the Llandudno hospital thought that Linda was Polish and did not speak nor understand a word of English, the poor old dear.

Obviously it did not matter to Linda while she was being operated upon, and while she was sleeping it off in the intensive care unit. But when she came to, she was first

140

bewildered and then infuriated. Why was everybody miming and gesticulating at her as if she was deaf?

Finally, she managed to get hold of a nurse's finger and squeeze it hard enough to make the girl bend over her.

'What is this?' she asked in a funny croaking whisper. 'A flipping madhouse?'

'It's okay, everybody,' said the nurse, 'she's English all right.'

—————————————— 7 ——————————————

It was very fortunate that nobody knew how much and for how long Linda Strizlik/Wren had been fiddling with her cut of the universe, eliciting her mother's praise and evoking other ghosts alien to these coasts.

Not even John Brett could have guessed how very fortunate it was that he did not feel like making love to Linda that afternoon, that he left her bed in time to meet the yet – and ever after – unsuspecting Angharad.

Not only was he thus kept out of any harm: the damage to the entire valley was kept to a minimum. Another orgasm could have made Linda oblivious to the true facts of life; in which case the ghost of her mother would have stayed, and what with the weather running amok anyway, it could all have resulted in an earthquake and a tidal wave on top of a hurricane.

But seriously: there can be no doubt that when Linda finished her pages, when she went and sat on the rock looking at the sea and the horizon and declared herself indelibly a loving woman, the universe heaved a sigh of relief.

The whirlwind may have been a result of this, but it was not such a stupendous price to demand, and pay. The only human being seriously hurt was Linda. Only about a dozen sheep were found dead, and Angharad's white cow. A few barns collapsed, and there was some damage to practically every roof in the valley, but the only building that caught fire and was destroyed beyond repair was Owen's *hafodty*. The birds, apart from some very late eggs and retarded fledgelings, survived unharmed. The saddest loss was the trees, the beautiful tall solitary ones; the scruffy pine forest looked scruffier yet but unhurt.

And there was, of course, the rain to make up for the losses. Every spring stream and well rose, and if the water was muddy at first, it soon cleared itself and tasted as it had in the good old times before pollution. The bogs splashed and smacked and bubbled under every footstep, just as they should. The grass went mad and to Angharad's delight grew on sight, lush and luscious. The rain came down solidly for three days and three nights and after that it simply rained on and off, just as expected of a climate that was neither too kind nor too unkind.

In the end, everybody was happy and it never occurred to anyone to blame anything on Linda Strizlik/Wren.

The Owens collected a rather unsatisfactory sum from their insurance company, but Angharad made it up to them by buying the scorched but solid walls from them. She and John were planning to roof them over and use the structure as a cowshed. With the trees gone, the cattle would need a shelter from the heat and rain. Richard mourned all the odd books and old dictionaries that went up in the blaze; Honorah wept over sweet memories connected with the place, and over Richard who seemed to be growing so old and fidgety and was seeing things out of all proportion.

Like when he insisted on flying to Llandudno and got terribly angry that no such flight was available, as if he had not known all his life! On the train, he kept telling everybody what a wonderful woman Linda Wren was, a witness really, and how important such people were if British culture was not to remain insular. He quoted liberally from Kafka, sometimes even in German – Honorah had always held his German in low esteem – until he drove half the carriage away. Then he fell asleep, leaving Honorah to ponder the rather agonizing questions of what the deuce were they supposed to do about the woman! What – if anything – had been expected of them by the hospital people, or Linda herself?

But it turned out to be quite a pleasurable week. They saw Linda several times, briefly at first, but after she had been transferred from the intensive care unit into a spacious ward they were allowed to bring her fruit and little treats and sit longer by her bed.

The doctors and nurses were very fond of this cheerful, smiling, uncomplaining woman whose injuries were extensive and painful; her visitors were treated with special courtesy, even by the matron. One of the doctors asked Richard Owen to autograph his recent book on Kafka for him; and another turned out to be a brother of Honorah's best-ever student who had graduated last year. The chief surgeon had assured them that there was no danger of Miss Wren being left crippled or anything. And Linda herself gave a thrilling description of the storm, so vivid that it felt as if they had been there. On the whole, it was all most entertaining, and pleasingly charitable, and there were no strings attached.

Between visits, the Owens were staying at the farm with Angharad, her mother, the two boys, and John Brett. The big question that kept popping up during each meal was whether John and Angharad should delay the wedding until Linda got better, or whether they ought to get married regardless.

Richard was for the first alternative. Honorah, who was a woman of sound instincts, could not see why Linda should be expected to enjoy the wedding, and advised the two lovebirds to go ahead.

She did so time and again, until it became clear that this was exactly what John and Angharad had wanted to do anyway. The truth established, they both blushed crimson, simultaneously. Like twins, really, though one's hair was the colour of a raven, the other's of a fox.

Scavengers, both, was a terribly unkind thought that flashed through Honorah's mind. She shrank from it, but just at that very moment Dick sought her hand under the table and squeezed it hard. If what Dick and I have is not love, mused Honorah, what is?

'Would you do me a favour?' asked Linda who, at the end

of the week, was already sitting up, even though propped by a large pillow and ridiculously square in her plaster cast.

'Anything,' replied the Owens in unison.

'Would you write a note to my daughter in Paris? I've tried, but the fingers of my right hand won't move properly, the five little pips. And all I could ever do with my left hand was hold a cigarette!'

'Of course,' said the Owens in unison and Honorah laughed, solo. 'We've been doing this for a week, isn't it awful? You'd think we'd lived together for a couple of centuries!'

'Would you tell her . . . oh, I don't know. I wish she'd come over and see me. I'd give her the money, but I can't give her the time . . . the desire.'

'You leave it to me,' declared Honorah, her chin set.

'Just what I was about to say,' nodded Dick, 'leave it to Honey. We may not look it, but we have grown-up children of our own, you know.'

'Didn't trust my spelling, eh, love?' said Linda's neighbour to the right after the Owens had departed. 'Can't say I blame you! I've always been getting it wrong, my maths too, my mum used to say that I must have a sieve where she's got brains.'

She was a painfully thin woman with a bandaged head and a dark bruise on her cheek; she kept fingering and scratching it.

'My mum,' she chuckled, 'bless her, used to get really annoyed with me. You know what she would say? She'd say that they must have swopped the babies in the maternity ward where I was born, in Chester that was. She'd say I was brought in from a gypsy wagon and that the gypsies had taken my brains out and eaten them. I used to howl something awful, I believed every word my mum said, I didn't know any better, being so stupid and all that. And look at me now!'

She fingered her bruise fondly and chuckled again. 'I don't mean this, this is just an accident. Love, you're looking

145

at the first self-employed independent woman plumber in the whole of Llandudno!'

'Well done,' said Linda.

'What's your mum been like when you was little?' asked the woman in a curiously childish voice.

'I don't know,' sighed Linda. 'A bit on the cold side, I think. I can't remember much . . . looks like I must have a sieve where you've got brains!'

'It's the shock. It gets to you. I know!' She sounded competent again, and very friendly. 'Shall I tell you about my accident?'

Frantishka hated the Eiffel Tower from the depths of her heart. It wasn't too bad to look at from a distance, but it gave her the shivers whenever she was forced to come near it. Standing underneath was possibly the worst. All that ironmongery looming and booming overhead, all those lifts sliding up and down its legs like swollen bugs, the endless strings of tiny people treading the staircases, looking black against the sky, like ants. Frantishka had always had a thing about ants.

And she did not enjoy looking at Paris from up above; the perspective wasn't kind to Paris, it made her look like any other overgrown overstuffed city splayed from horizon to horizon.

But she wasn't here to look at anything. She was taken up because Jean-Pierre wanted the wind in her hair and the sky behind her head – *le ciel vibrant de printemps* – for yet another series of publicity photographs. '*Mon Dieu, comme tu es belle!*' he said whenever he looked at her through the lens.

Frantishka had abandoned the idea of going to a nunnery only a couple of months ago, but she had already moved across the full scale of a girl's possibilities. She was about to become a film actress, possibly a movie star: it probably had to happen, she had that kind of beauty, and she photographed extremely well.

Jean-Pierre was moving her from *gauche* to *droit, un peu, un peu plus*, and encouraged *petite* conversations to keep her looking natural. '*Tu vas donc en Angleterre?* he'd ask. '*Ta mère, est-ce qu'elle est belle aussi? Elle même? Comme toi?*'

'*Elle est différente,*' said Frantishka, and thought oh no, she isn't a bit like me, and you would not find her beautiful. I used to think that she was the most beautiful woman on earth, until . . . oh I don't know, until I was about ten, I suppose. I want to see her. She's been hurt, I want to go to her. I have not loved her enough, not since she took me away from dad. I want to love her. And even if I can't, I want to pretend I love her. I want her to see me loving her.

'*Parfait!*' exclaimed Jean-Pierre. '*C'est drôle, ça, mais tu es encore plus belle quand tu es triste!*'

A new woman was wheeled into the ward from the intensive care unit. Her face was hidden behind bandages like a mummy's and her breath was coming through the slits so unevenly and noisily that it sounded as if she were singing.

'You know, I believe she is,' said matron to Linda and her neighbour. 'If you listen properly, there is a melody. She is our mystery patient, nobody knows who she is or where she came from. The police found her on the beach, she had not a stitch on, her face was all smashed in, and her ribcage, as if some maniac had been thumping up and down on her. Couldn't talk even if she wanted to. She could say a word or two now, but no, she won't, and if you put a pen into her hand, she just drops it.'

'Looks like a campaign against women and their heads,' exclaimed Linda's neighbour. 'I mean, look at us! I ask you, matron, is this normal?'

She was right. Every one of the eight women in the ward had – apart from other injuries – her head bandaged, one way or other.

'Hush!' Linda raised her hand and listened intently, leaning forward as much as her plaster would allow.

They all held their breath. In the sudden silence, the woman's breathing sounded eerily like music.

'I believe it's an old Russian song, matron,' said Linda quietly, 'and I think I am right.'

'Well, I certainly hope that she will prove to be as much

Russian as you proved to be Polish,' said matron rather coldly. Then she remembered the picture postcard and her face lit up. Childless herself, she liked people to have children. She took the postcard out of her pocket and held it high.

'Who is a dear mum, then?' she sang out. 'From Paris, too! Fancy that! Who is the lucky young devil? A boy or a girl?'

Linda sat up all night and was feverish and poorly in the morning.

Ruth and Alice came to see Linda that afternoon and were appalled to see her looking so ill, so visibly hurt.

'You old fool,' sighed Ruth and began to peel an orange.

'Poor Linda,' added Alice, frowning at Ruth.

'Poor Linda, boo boo,' fumed Ruth. 'I can't stand you when you are being a hypocrite, Alice. What was it you said after we got that postcard from Linda? Shall I tell you? I know what you said, because it gave me the shivers. You looked like a witch. "She'll pay for this," you said, "she'll pay!"'

'So she has,' purred Alice, smoothing out Linda's brow with her little finger, 'so she has. Everything is all right now. Everything's fine.'

After that, they had long lovely minutes together, a flutter of light touches, quick little words, brief loving glances from under the eyelashes, and long gentle looks. Until Alice sat up straight:

'Well, are you coming back to us, or are you moving in with him?'

'Him who?' Linda was genuinely astonished.

'Don't say that there wasn't a man behind all this flight to nature!'

'There wasn't!'

'For three long months you have been alone in an isolated cottage on a mountain. There was absolutely no man.'

'Oh. No, I can't say that.'

148

Ruth leaned eagerly forward and clapped her hands. 'Oh goodie! Who is he, Linda? Where is he?'

'Gone with the wind,' said Linda wearily and shut her eyes to stop the probing. She was beginning to feel utterly exhausted. Loving is tiresome.

The woman with no face started to sing again with her breath. It was a horrible sound, droning and moaning, but the melody was there, bo-i-led chi-cken, fri-e-d chi-cken, it was pulling at Linda's heart-strings, dragging her down, down, down.

'Jesus!' said Ruth feelingly. 'Who is she?'

Linda was moving her lips and Ruth bent over to catch the whisper.

'What did she say?' asked Alice.

'I don't know. It sounded like "I – sister". She looks frightfully bad, Alice.'

'Maybe she wanted us to call the sister!'

The sister came and took Linda's pulse. 'I am afraid you will have to leave now. She is not at all well.'

Linda was transferred back to the intensive care unit. She spent most of the night staring at the ceiling and when she finally fell asleep, she immediately developed a dream.

Ruth, her eyes sparkling with mischief and her hair done in girlish curls, took Linda by the hand and led her through a high door into a large building. Inside, there was the unmistakable combination of polished wood, glass, green cloth and cheap marble; of hushed-up voices and sharp echoes of hurried footsteps; of draught and stuffiness; of anxiety and giggles: it was a school.

Ruth had pushed her into a roomy, untidy cabinet and shut the door. There were some teachers about, all women, who nodded to Linda with friendly smiles. It became clear that she was to look for clues to find Alice, that despite Ruth's appearance this had nothing to do with childhood, that they were all adult women sharing a gentle joke, a birthday perhaps.

There was a bottle of wine, all wrapped up in a white dressing material, underneath a washbasin; on the soap dish, a neat fold of beautiful gift-wrapping paper; inside, a white card which said 'Go to the lab.' Linda went through a good many corridors, classrooms and cabinets, met many young women who smiled, but found no lab.

The last shabby door brought her out onto the street again. Oh, but that was clever: she would cross to the pavement opposite to gain some distance and look for such windows as would betray a laboratory. Which she did, and soon spotted Alice standing by one of the windows, larger than life, and smiling. But there was something else; Alice's face, if looked at properly, was flushed with anger or pain, the smile was a sneer; actually it wasn't Alice's face at all and Linda didn't want to know whose it was, no, and the nurse came with a thermometer and was surprised at the depth of Linda's thanks. Any time, she laughed; but the patient's temperature had gone up again, the doctors came, and the day began.

Just before noon, the woman plumber sneaked in on her way back from the X-rays. She was brimming with news.

'Listen, she's gone!'

'Who?' Linda's eyes opened up with hope.

'The mummy! She just up and went, some time during the night! You should see the mess down there. The nurses are snivelling, the sister's had hysterics, matron runs thunderbolting around, the police are going from bed to bed. Nobody's seen anything. They are still searching the hospital, and the town. Imagine, a mummy like that in a short hospital gown that opens up on her arse, barefoot, singing, and nobody's seen anything!'

'Nobody's told me anything!'

'That's what I thought. I knew you'd be glad to know that she'd gone. I saw the way she was getting on your nerves. You mustn't let things get to you the way you do!'

'Thank you. I won't.'

'Poor devil. I wonder who she was. A loony. Women! We're all loonies. All women are mad!'

Linda burst out laughing and a nurse came and chased her friend away. But Linda went on chuckling for most of the day, slept well, and all her functions returned to normal. Next morning, an orderly came to wheel her back to the ward and she asked for a chair rather than the cart. After a brief consultation with the doctor, a wheelchair was brought in and the orderly pushed it gently along the corridors. Sitting up, Linda felt much more dignified, and from this proper perspective the hospital looked ten times more cheerful.

'You do keep us busy, don't you,' said the orderly meaningfully, and Linda promised him a fiver if he took her to the pay-phone, dialled a London number for her and kept feeding the coins in.

Things one can be grateful for, thought Linda who just couldn't wipe the smile off her face, like how lovely that it is my left arm and my left ear that are bandaged in, and not my left arm and right ear, or right arm and left ear; that would take a lot of pleasure out of a telephone conversation.

'Could I speak to Dr B., please? – Wren. Miss Linda Wren. – Hi. – It's me all right. – Of course you would. My accent is my own, like my fingerprints. – I am fine! I am beautifully fine. I've never been better. – I am sorry. I will. – Not quite so soon, but I will. I'll come at the happy hour. Cocktail time. – Have you got a patient with you? – I see. But don't you worry, you may run out of business one day, but you'll never run out of research material! That's the good news I am actually calling you about. And I've got it from an independent, self-employed person; it's reliable. – Here goes: we are all loonies. Women. All women are mad! – That's it, what more do you want? – I've got to go now. Give the couch a pat from me. – Yes. Thank you. Bye!'

'Who was it?' asked the orderly. 'A shrink? I wouldn't trust him.'

'I don't,' said Linda, 'but I liked him a lot.'

'The trouble with your mother, *ma jolie*,' Ben Strizlik was

saying to his daughter, who was steering a beautifully recon-
ditioned Volkswagen Beetle along the motorway, 'the
trouble with your mother is that she has lost face. She thinks
she is so English, right? Well, she isn't. She is still one of
those soft weepy Czechs who'd faint if you said communism,
revolution or Soviet Union. Democratic socialism! It's like
having your cake and eating it too. Believe me, I know them.
They build sandcastles right by a mighty ocean and then
weep when they get swept away by the tide. They like to
suffer, actually, if they can keep the suffering warm and
cosy. Your mother should have suffered it out with them.
She should never have come to England. We would have
managed, you and I and your grandma.'

They were approaching Birmingham, and Frantishka
swerved the little car into an exit lane.

'Hey! Why don't you stay on the motorway, darling?'

'I'm sorry, dad. I'm driving you to the station. You're
going back to Portsmouth.'

'What have I done?'

'I just don't want you with me. It's all been a mistake. I
don't think mum would want to see you.'

'I'd wait outside.'

'No. I'm sorry.'

'Are you so terribly offended by what I said about the
Czechs? I keep forgetting that there's a charming little half
of you that's Czech.'

'No, dad. For that I merely pitied you. You'd say any
screaming nonsense that would make you feel superior,
wouldn't you? No, it's what you said about mum. You know
I've always begrudged her taking me away from you? I
never knew you actually wanted her to stay behind! Never
to come and be with me! Jesus!'

'I didn't mean it quite that way. I was thinking of her,
not you. She could have been happier, you know.'

'Without me? Do shut up, dad. Out you go. I'll take you
to dinner on my way back. You're in luck. I don't un-love
easily.'

Frantishka was allowed to wheel her mother out into the

little park inside the hospital walls. The lawns were luscious, the roses were in full first bloom, the seagulls were swooping down from the clear June sky, the leaves were flitting and twinkling on the trees, and there was a policeman patrolling the grounds, looking into the bushes and under the benches. Apparently a long strip of bandage had been found on a rosebush that morning; nothing so very unusual in a hospital, but the search for the mystery woman was renewed just in case.

Linda didn't let it worry her. She was puffing away on a Gauloise and the feel of it was overwhelming, it felt like being scrubbed clean inside out with tobacco-flavoured sandpaper. Frantishka was talking, and Linda listened to her vibrant, warbling voice with wonder in her heart, with humble happiness, and with wild, savage, sky-storming pride: my daughter, free like a bird, and beautiful.

They had a good many laughs together, mainly at the kind of language Frantishka was using, Czech, English and French all bubbling like a cocktail spurting from a shaker. It would have offended any linguistic purist, or any Czech, English or French patriot, but it was a delight to their ears and it took the holiness out of their communion.

Frantishka spent the night in a hotel, came back in the morning, and they did the whole thing all over again, roses, Gauloises, laughter and all – only the policeman was missing.

When the time came to part, Frantishka said, 'I like you, mum, I like you a lot.'

'Listen, honey,' pleaded Linda, 'don't let them mess you up with too much make-up. Go for the naked face. Be beautiful.'

'You sound just like Jean-Pierre,' laughed Frantishka.

'I sound just like somebody you don't know,' sighed Linda. 'A man I met.'

Frantishka blushed deeply. 'I'm a virgin, mum. That's bad news, isn't it?'

'Fiddlesticks. It's a beautiful thing to start life with. Or end up with. Look at me – with a little luck, I'll be a virgin again.'

'Mum. . . .' Frantishka hesitated.

'I know. You don't have to write. I won't, much. I wonder why it is so much easier to write letters to men. Send me a postcard now and then, but not the horrid Eiffel Tower again, I hate it!'

'Mum *chérie, muminka* dear, I think I love you,' said Frantishka and flew away, high into the sky, fiery and swift like a kestrel, bright like a star, a morning star, a Françoise Roitelet, a little wren with a far-fetching voice.

'Goodness me,' sighed Linda's friend, the woman plumber, 'isn't she beautiful? And glamorous. I know she's your daughter and all that, but don't you feel what I feel? Why the hell can't we all be beautiful? It wouldn't matter then if we were loonies, would it!'

'Here, have a Gauloise,' offered Linda, 'that'll scrub it out of you. It works with me.'

'Scrub out what?'

'The envy,' said Linda, and the two women wrapped in bizarre bandages and striped hospital gowns smoked like chimneys until the bell rang and they had to leave the park, the one wheeling the other in, the blind leading the deaf, or possibly the other way around.

Frantishka did take her father, senior lecturer at Portsmouth Polytechnic Ben Strizlik, out to dinner. She had already forgiven him what there was to forgive, and suppressed the rest.

She crossed the Channel and exposed her Czech, English, Austrian and Jewish bones to the French cameras. The director liked her very much.

'*Françoise*,' he asked, '*es-tu absolument sûre que tu n'es pas Russe?*'

'*Absolument*,' laughed Frantishka, she was absolutely sure that she was not Russian. There weren't very many things she could be sure of, but this was one of them. Not that she would have minded; she had just acquired a taste for Pushkin and thought that if the Russians were both exuberant and sentimental and rather cruelly obsessed with beauty and prettiness, and painfully patriotic, so were the French. And anyway, Frantishka wouldn't have minded belonging to any people whatever. She was free. For that very reason, she became quite an active young member of the Ligue pour les Droits des Hommes.

If, in addition, she could save some of the money she was going to earn for her old age, hers could be a fine life and would make lovely memoirs. Linda would have a small, touching place in them, as mothers should.

John Brett brought Linda a gift. After the layer of ashes three feet deep inside the *hafodty*'s walls had finally been washed away by the rains, he found a key amongst the debris scattered on the scorched ground. It had melted around the edges and twisted into a curious shape, like a crouching man or woman. John had rubbed it clean and polished it and attached it to a string of tiny seashells; it made a beautiful present.

He kept glancing at his watch, and Linda had to help him escape by pretending that it was time for her afternoon nap. She watched him stride away and twinged with pain, and jealousy, and an ancient, bottomless sorrow. Patience, heart, patience!

When he was no longer in sight, peace came to Linda, and a quiet anticipation. The ransom had been paid, the hostage released, the ordinary flow of life was pushing in. 'You'll heal,' whispered a knowing voice, and it was Linda's neighbour to the right, the independent woman plumber.

She was called Judith Kowalski but actually came from an old and impoverished Irish family. She had been discharged from the hospital long before Linda was fit to leave, but she came to see her regularly. She would pop in just after lunch; in the early hours of each evening she would sit with Linda in the park and wrest the story of her life out of her hesitant mouth; she was insatiably curious, and unswervingly sympathetic.

Judith had four brothers: one was living in Aberdeen, one in Derry, one in Exeter, and the youngest had emigrated to Australia. She had always wanted a sister: now here was a candidate if she ever saw one, ready-made and in need of help.

If everything was carefully plotted, and properly organized, the two of them could make a life out of one living. Linda could take over the paperwork, and the cleaning up after the job had been done, maybe she'd even learn a trick or two with the tools. But Judith wasn't saying anything yet, not out loud; she didn't want to alarm Linda. Wasn't she just like a bird which had gone on a passage with the wrong flock, got its instincts all mixed up, lost its sense of destination, and landed right in Judith's lap?

Judith had been happily married twice, and twice she had let the man go, because she could not bear him children. After that she set her teeth and learned her trade. She was indestructible, sociable and lonely.

'Come on love, give us a smile,' pleaded Judith. 'There's more to you than sour grapes! Remember, a woman's soul is in her face, or so my mum used to say, may she rest in peace.'

'What do you know,' laughed Linda, 'so did mine! Did she scrub your face with a wet towel before sending you to school? Or, in shops and places, did she spit on her handkerchief and rub the corners of your mouth with it?'

Judith shuddered. 'You bet she did. Proves we all come from the same unhappy breed, doesn't it? Listen, have you ever done it to your daughter?' Linda shook her head and Judith sighed. 'There *is* progress, then.'

'Judith . . . after they let me out of here . . . I was wondering, could I . . . could you. . . .'

'What d'you know,' grinned Judith and began to peel an orange. 'I think we could give it a try.'

'What if we are too different politically?' fretted Linda.

'How on earth could we be?' said Judith.

The mystery of the singing mummy was never properly solved, but at least the people of Llandudno could cease being frightened of seeing her suddenly in the dark. Blood-stained bandages were found on the beach, yards and yards of them, and the blood group matched that of the nameless patient who had vanished from the hospital.

Legends were told, of course. There were such as swore that they'd seen a strange boat sailing away from the beach, with a huge red lantern hanging high on the mast, on the dark moonless night before they found the bandages. There was a fisherman who told a story about a dolphin or a torpedo or some other thing so shaped carrying a woman on its back in the early hours of the morning. He said that the woman's face was awesomely scarred but peaceful, and he also said that she turned and waved at him, but that was widely disbelieved.

Then there was a party of early and elderly holidaymakers from Manchester who were showing their bruised legs and arms around the town. They said that they were jogging alongside the beach at about seven in the morning and were a good two miles or so from the camp when they were suddenly and violently thrown against the sea wall by a gush of wind that came from the south, hit the beach, whirled around and vanished in the south again, carrying a dark, inscrutable, cloudy mass of sand with it. Anything could have been hidden in it, anything.

In view of the recent freak storm that had hit the Croesor valley many people in Llandudno, the police included, were inclined to take this for the most plausible explanation of the woman's, or her corpse's, disappearance. But on the whole the fisherman's story was much preferred. He was a local man, and his story could be interpreted at leisure in terms of Russian submarines, mad scientists, mermaids, or aliens from faraway disturbing planets.

As All Souls' Eve approached, Linda, as usual, was getting restless.

'It isn't right,' declared Judith, 'that anybody should be kept away from their family's graves. What is the matter with you, love? Are you, or aren't you, going to do something about it?'